Praise for *Coal Black Horse*

"Gorgeous and moving. . . . With his lush, incantatory voice, Robert Olmstead describes a boy thrust into one of the war's most horrific moments."   —*The Washington Post Book World*

"With a horse like this, you just want to ride. And with the descriptive power such as he displays here, Olmstead makes the ride an exciting one—in lean prose, reminiscent of Crane's *Red Badge of Courage,* with just the proper amount of sharp description. The special flavor Olmstead lends to the tale seems to come from a mix of ancient myth and our bloody history."
     —NPR's *All Things Considered*

"A singular and poetic addition to the Civil War bookshelf. Like E. L. Doctorow's award-winning *The March,* Robert Olmstead's sixth novel ripples with with vivid war scenes and rich characterizations."   —*The Atlanta Journal-Constitution*

"Magisterial. . . . *Coal Black Horse* is a remarkable creation. . . . Rife with the shattering lessons of war."   —*Chicago Tribune*

"A riveting tale of the American past and a brilliantly realized journey into the heart of darkness. . . . It's the kind of storytelling that you will want to read once simply for the storytelling. . . . Then you will want to read it again to let Olmstead's prose wash over you. It's as muscular, sturdy, well hewn, and wise as the coal-black horse himself."   —*The Boston Globe*

"Gripping. . . . A mesmerizing, timely look at what war does to all of us. In stark, simple language, and a grammatical structure that echoes the work of Cormac McCarthy, Olmstead has found his own voice, one you will not easily forget."

—*The Cleveland Plain Dealer*

"In no-frills prose, Olmstead deftly unspools Robey's too-early loss of innocence and harrowing passage to manhood."

—*Entertainment Weekly*

"Exciting. . . . A grueling adventure."

—*The New York Times Book Review*

"Carries readers along as easily as the powerful, cunning coal black horse carries Robey Childs. . . . A taut, elegant novel of nearly flawless tone and structure—sweepingly descriptive, chock-full of unforgettable characters, authenticized with coarse country dialogue, satisfying on many levels. . . . A remarkable story of redemption carried on the strong back of masterful storytelling."

—*Chicago Sun-Times*

"*Coal Black Horse* takes on the sheen of another Civil War masterpiece, *The Red Badge of Courage*. Like Stephen Crane's classic, Olmstead's book is a harrowing tale of wartime horrors and deep human struggles, all sown within the American soil and spirit."

—*The Miami Herald*

"Olmstead's voice is clear, precise and vivid. . . Civil War buffs entraced by *Cold Mountain* will find *Coal Black Horse* a gallant equal."

—MSNBC.com

"Olmstead's powerful, spare novel takes a romantic tale of chivalry (a young knight, his horse, and a quest) and distorts it through the nightmare lens of war." —*The Christian Science Monitor*

"Olmstead makes the ride an exciting one, with just enough lean prose to keep the mystery an event both in time and out . . . and just the proper amount of sharp description to keep us bound to whatever piece of earth the particular moment of the story happens to be grounded in. . . . An effective mix of stark classic narrative and uncloying nostalgia." —*San Francisco Chronicle*

"A harrowing tale of wartime horrors and redemption set amid the gore and carnage that was the American Civil War. . . . Olmstead follows his true narrative voice and writes like a man on fire." —*The Denver Post*

"Compelling. . . . Suspenseful plotting, meticulous historical research and . . . equally lyrical descriptions of nature and violence." —*The Charlotte Observer*

"A powerful tale of the loss of innocence and the madness of war." —*Richmond Times-Dispatch*

"A gripping read, with much extremely vivid rendering. . . . Sex, violence, revenge, sympathetic young protagonist, maiden in distress . . . it's all there, enveloped in a plausibly dark take on life and death." —*The San Diego Union-Tribune*

"Both moving and inspirational. The tale also becomes a meditation on what war does to a man's soul."
—*Milwaukee Journal Sentinel*

"Profound. . . . Mesmerizing."   —*The Columbus Dispatch*

"Robert Olmstead has created a compelling and beautifully written story that matches poetic and gritty writing with a page-turning plot."   —*The Tampa Tribune*

"A haunting portrayal of the madness of war and its corrosive effects."   —*The Salt Lake Tribune*

"The book's powerful message lingers like the smell of wood smoke from a mountaintop cabin or an army encampment. The simplicity and endurance of the central characters leave the reader moved by the enormity of courage in a landscape of waste."   —*The Star Democrat* (Maryland)

"*Coal Black Horse* is so tightly constructed that not a ray of sunshine pierces the solemn sky. The parched prose is black, brown, and gray exisiting within a world turned upside-down. Olmstead's skill is considerable."   —*Biloxi Sun Herald*

"A classic, timely tale of the cost of war, and the tragic toll it takes on individuals and their families."   —*The Missourian*

"A stark, brutally lyrical Civil War novel."
                —*The Memphis Commercial Appeal*

COAL BLACK HORSE

Also by Robert Olmstead

River Dogs
Soft Water
A Trail of Heart's Blood Wherever We Go
America by Land
Stay Here with Me

COAL BLACK HORSE

Robert Olmstead

ALGONQUIN BOOKS OF CHAPEL HILL | 2008

Published by
ALGONQUIN BOOKS OF CHAPEL HILL
Post Office Box 2225
Chapel Hill, North Carolina 27515-2225

a division of
Workman Publishing
225 Varick Street
New York, New York 10014

First paperback edition, Algonquin Books of Chapel Hill, May 2008.
Originally published by Algonquin Books of Chapel Hill in 2007.
Printed in the United States of America.
Published simultaneously in Canada by Thomas Allen & Son Limited.
Design by April Leidig-Higgins.

Library of Congress Cataloging-in-Publication Data
Olmstead, Robert.
Coal black horse / Robert Olmstead.—1st ed.
p. cm.
ISBN-13: 978-1-56512-521-6 (HC)
1. Fathers and sons—Fiction. 2. United States—History—Civil War,
1861–1865—Fiction. I. Title.
PS3565.L67C63 2007
813'.54—dc22   2006042914

Scholastic Book Fair Edition
ISBN-13: 978-1-56512-623-7

Hast thou given the horse strength?

Hast thou clothed his neck with thunder?

He swalloweth the ground with fierceness and rage . . .

—BOOK OF JOB

1

T HE EVENING OF SUNDAY May 10 in the year 1863, Hettie Childs called her son, Robey, to the house from the old fields where he walked the high meadow along the fence lines where the cattle grazed, licking shoots of new spring grass that grew in the mowing on the edge of the pasture.

He walked a shambling gait, his knees to and fro and his shoulders rocking. His hands were already a man's hands, cut square, with tapering fingers, and his hair hung loose to his shoulders. He was a boy whose mature body would be taller yet and of late he'd been experiencing frightening spurts of growth. On one night alone he grew an entire inch and when morning came he felt stretched and his body ached and he cried out when he sat up.

The dogs scrambled to their feet and his mother asked what ailed him that morning. Of late she'd become impatient with the inexplicit needs of boys and men and their acting so rashly on what they could not fathom and surely could not articulate. In her mind, men were no different than droughty weather or a sudden burst of rainless storm. They came and they went; they ached and pained. They laughed privately and cried to themselves as if heeding a way-off silent call. They were forever childish, sweet and convulsive. They heard sound the way dogs heard sound. They were like the moon — they changed every eight days.

He scratched at his head, knotting his long hair with his fingers. He felt to have been seized by phantoms in the night and twisted and turned, and his body spasmed and contorted.

He told her that he did not know exactly what it was possessed him, and did not even understand what happened enough to be dumb about it, but thought it was a condition, like all others, that was not significant and with patience it soon would pass.

"That seems about right," she said.

As he walked the fence lines that cold, silky spring evening, he let a hickory stick rattle along the silvered split rails. He was thinking about his father gone to war. Always his father, always just a thought, a word, a gesture away. He spoke aloud to him in his absence. He asked him questions and made observations. He said good night to him before he fell asleep and good morning when he woke up. He thought it would not be strange to see him around a corner, sitting on a stool, anytime, soon, now. He had been born on the mountain in the room where his mother and father conceived him, but it was his father who insisted he was not really a born-baby but a discovered-baby and was found swimming in the cistern, sleeping in the strawy manger, squatting on an orange pumpkin, behind the cowshed.

Swarming the air about his head that evening, there was a cloud of newly hatched mayflies, ephemeral and chaffy, their pale membrous wings pleating the darkening sky. Not an hour ago he'd watched them ascend in their moment, like a host of angels from the stream that bubbled from a split rock and pooled, before scribing a silver arc in the boulder-strewn pasture, before falling over a cliff, and then he heard his mother's plaintive voice.

When he came down from the high meadow, the dogs were standing sentry at her sides, their solemn stalky bodies leaning into her.

She said softly and then she said again with the conclusion of all time in her voice when he did not seem to understand, "Thomas Jackson has died."

"It is now over," she said, not looking at him, not favoring his eyes, but looking past him and some place beyond. There was no emotion in her words. There was no sign for him to read that would reveal the particulars of her inner thoughts. Her face was the composure of one who had experienced the irrevocable. It was a fact unalterable and it was as simple as that.

He held his bony wrist in his opposite hand. He shuffled his feet as if that gesture were a means to understanding. He patiently waited because he knew when she was ready, she would tell him what this meant.

"Thomas Jackson has been killed," she finally said. "There's no sense in this continuing." She paused and sought words to fashion her thoughts. "This was a mistake a long time before we knew it, but a mistake nonetheless. Go and find your father and bring him back to his home."

Her words were as if come through time and she was an old mother and the ancient woman.

"Where will I find him?" he asked, unfolding his shoulders and setting his feet that he might stand erect.

"Travel south," she said. "Then east into the valley and then north down the valley."

She had sewed for him an up-buttoned, close-fitting linen
shell jacket with the braids of a corporal and buttons made of
sawed and bleached chicken bones. She told him it was imperative that he leave the home place this very night and not
to dally along the way but to find his father as soon as he
could and to surely find him by July.

"You must find him before July," she said.

He was not to give up his horse under any circumstance
whatsoever and if confronted by any man, he was to say he
was a courier and he was to say it fast and to be in a hurry and
otherwise to stay hush and learn what he needed to know by
listening, like he was doing right now. She then told him there
is a terror that men bring to the earth, to its water and air and
its soil, and he would meet these men on his journey and that
his father was one of these men, and then she paused and
studied a minute and then she told him, without judgment,
that someday he too might become one of these men.

"Be aware of who you take help from," she told him, "and
who you don't take help from." Then she eyed him coldly and
told him, to be safe, he must not take help from anyone.

"Don't trust anyone," she said. "Not man, nor woman nor
child."

The jacket on the one side was dun gray in color, dyed of
copperas and walnut shells. When she turned it inside out, it
showed blue with similar braids of rank. She told him he was
to be on whatever side it was necessary to be on and not to
trust either side.

"Secure pistols," she said, "and do this as soon as you can.
Gain several and keep them loaded at all times. If you must
shoot someone, shoot for the wide of their body, and when

one pistol is empty throw it away and gain the pistol of the man you have shot. If you think someone is going to shoot you, then trust they are going to shoot you and you are to shoot them first."

Her voice did not rise. It betrayed no panic. She instructed him with calmness and determination, as if the moment she'd anticipated had finally arrived and she was saying words to him she had decided upon a long time ago.

"Yes ma'am," he said quietly, and repeated her words back to her. "Shoot them first."

The dogs shivered and mewled and clacked their jaws.

"Remember," she said, reaching her hands to his shoulders, "danger passes by those who face up to it."

He remembered too how she had told him at twelve years of age he was old enough to work the land, but he wasn't old enough to die for it. To die for the land, he had to be at least fourteen years old and now he was.

When she finished her instructions, he drew a bucket of icy water from the well and splashed himself down to the waist. He toweled himself dry and unfolded a clean linen shirt. He dressed in black bombazine trousers and a pair of his father's flat-heeled leather brogans and then he donned the shell jacket. His square hands and bony wrists extended beyond the jacket's cuffs while the trouser legs gathered at his shoe tops. He plucked at his cuffs and tugged at the bones to make room for his chest.

His mother observed to him that he had growed some on top, as if it were a mystery to her and his face colored in patches for in her voice was carried a mother's tenderness, but for the most she remained distant and did not change her mind and did not suggest he eat and sleep and wait until morning light before he departed.

After a time, long and purposeful, she cast her eyes on him, but she did not gift him with her smile. She reached up and he bent down and she hesitantly touched him at the side of his face. Her fingertips lingered on his cheek and neck as if she were not one with eyesight but was a blinded woman seeing with her fingers, and then she held a button and tugged and he felt as if she was pulling the inside of his chest.

It was then he realized just how sad and how futile his journey was to be. She was sending him in the direction of his own death and she could see it in no other way and she could do nothing else than send him off. Even if he was to return alive, she'd never forgive herself for risking her son's life for the sake of his father's life.

"You take off the coat," she said, changing her mind, and she helped him free the buttons and shuck the coat sleeves from his shoulders and arms. "Be a boy as long as you can. It won't be that much longer. Then use the dyed coat. You will know when."

"Yes ma'am."

"You are not to die," she said, though in her face loomed darkness.

"No ma'am."

"You will be back," she said, her eyes suddenly alive, as if they were eyes seeing the life past this life.

"Yes ma'am. I will be back," he said, glancing toward the darkness of the open door.

"You will promise," she said, commanding his attention.

"I promise."

"Then I will wait here for you," she said, and reached her

other hand to his face and drew him to her as she raised her body to his and kissed his lips.

In that kiss was the single moment she reconsidered her imperative. It passed through her as if a hand of benediction. He waited for her to say more words to him, but she did not. He felt her blue eyes wetting his face. She kissed him again, more urgently this time, and they both knew she had to let him go and then she let him go. He stepped away, gave a final wave of his hand and then he left out the door.

Outside, in the cooling, anodyne air of the mountain reach, evening was fading into night. His mother's touch still warmed his neck, his lips still heated from her kiss. He bridled a cobby gray horse with pearly eyes, saddled up, and rode from the home place and down into the darkness that possessed the Copperhead Road. If he had looked back, he would not have seen his mother but the dogs sitting in the still open doorway, their cadent breathing slow and imperceptible.

It took half that night to leave the sanctuary of the home place, to leave the high meadow, the old fields, and descend the mountain switchbacks into the cold damp hollows and to leave the circuits of the hollows and ride through the river mists of the big bottom. The trees and ledges sheltered the starlight as he passed beneath them. The mountain night was uncommonly still and the moonlight eerily shuttered by drifting scud, but in unshrouded moments the moonlight broke through and found the hollows and in long moments he was bathed in its white light as if the hollows were not made of stone but were channels of mirrored glass. So bright was the light he could read the lines in his hands and the gritted swirls in his fingertips.

He was still a boy and held the boy's fascination for how

light penetrates darkness, how water freezes and ice melts, how life could be not at all and all at once. How some things last for years without ever existing. He thought if the world was truly round he always stood in the center. He thought, Spring is turning into summer and I am riding south to meet it. He thought how his father was a traveling man and ever since he was a child he too dreamt of traveling most of all and now he was and he felt a sense of the impending.

He let float in the dark air his free hand and then raised it up and reached to the sky where his fingers enfolded a flickering red star. The star was warm in his hand and beat with the pulse of a frog or a songbird held in your palm. He caressed the star and let it ride in his palm and then he carried the star to his mouth where it tasted like sugar before he swallowed it.

2

THAT MORNING OF HIS leaving there was no sunrise. There was no reddening in the eastern sky but rather a lessening of darkness from black to gray by degree. The dark hours played with the trilling calls and countercalls of wood frogs on the edges of ponds. A flock of blackbirds bound north traced the night sky with their arrowed wings. The ledges leaked thin runnels of trickling icy water. From somewhere deep in the sanctuary of the laurels a vigilant stag was belling the herd.

Those close-walled hollows were deep and cold and sepulchral. Their towering bore in and seemed poised to close. The switchbacks were wet and their path of stones was smooth and slippery, and more than once the cobby horse slid and each time she did he tightened his legs on her stout barrel affording her what small surety he could. But frightened, she would halt and leg-stiff refuse to take another step. He sat her patiently and spoke softly into her flicking ears and after a while she would snort and begin to move.

The path continued its falling for mile upon mile into the green of the rising springtime. He let his feet slip from the stirrups and he lay back until his head was over her croup. He could not imagine coming down this road in darkness and spring runoff, but tonight that's what he was doing.

To reach the bridge that morning was as if to return from a long journey that began beyond the rim of the world. Memory of his mother and the home place traveled with him in only the vaguest sense and his sudden concern was that if he crossed the bridge he would cease to remember them altogether. He turned in his saddle and looked back to the place where he'd come from. He angered over the distance, the fastness and the resistance of the home place. How could a night be so long? How could a few miles suddenly be so far? How could a place be so singular and so selfish as to deny itself to your mind once you have left it?

His eyes were wet and for reasons he could not name his chest throbbed. He wiped at his stinging eyes and cursed out in the darkness, but he did not know what he was cursing. Just a boy's last curse when he's told he has to do something. Even if the boy secretly wants to do that something, by nature he will curse the redirection of his will. Where before he had possessed time, now time was no longer his. He was being sent into the world and him now fourteen years old and so ignorant of its ways.

When he crossed the bridge the land opened and spread and lay flat as if a length of ribbon unfurled on a cobbled lane. On the densing air was the smell of leaf mold and opening buds. The sound of running water filled his ears and then receded and then increased again as he approached the junction of waters where the Twelve Mile doglegged and plunged into the turbulence of the Canaan. He continued southeasterly to the roar of the spring runoff and the boulders knocking in their chambered course.

He'd not slept or eaten the whole of that night and his body was weak and qualmish. The land continued its widening and already the cobby horse was becoming too tired for the journey ahead. She blew heavy and shivered. The stones in her path were drenched with dew and her bare feet struck with increased concussion. Then she stumbled and stopped altogether and would not go forward. She snorted and tossed her head, slinging froth from her bit chain into the air. He kicked his heels into her flanks and slapped her rump, but she was unyielding. She cocked her head and flicked her ears forward and then back where they stayed.

Then he heard what she was listening to—the pinging sound a hammer makes on an anvil. Ahead was the little timbering village where old Morphew's mercantile stood on the way to the Greenbrier. He let her stand and shake out a repetition of long shivers that rippled her hide and once she settled he dismounted. He stroked her soft cheek and blew air into her wide waffling nostrils until she tossed her boxy head.

Her mouth was worn raw and bleeding where she'd worried the bit through the night. He told her she was surely in a state and he understood why because he was in one too, but it was going to be all right. He leaned into her left shoulder and when she gave him her weight, he folded her leg up. Her foot was heated and tender and the frog bleeding where it was penetrated by a sliver of shale in the shape of an arrowhead. With his folding knife he removed the stone sliver and she was relieved, but the damage was done. He set her foot down and with a coaxing of words, he was able to lead her forward.

Now he heard the squealing eeek of the wooden frame that held the suspended bellows, the rattle of chain as the leathers expanded and collapsed, wheezing spurts of pumping air. The ground of the forge was strewn with plowshares and coulters. Beneath the worktable was a comb of grass and on top was a clutter of hammers, chisels, and punches.

The smith hovered over the fire, intent on the blue-straw color crawling up the metal from the depths of the forge. Then he turned at the shoulders and quenched it in a banging hiss of steam. The smith, a bent and hunchbacked German, had forged the iron hook that hung in their chimney. He pointed their turning plow. He made his mother's knitting needles.

One end of Old Morphew's porch was clasped in the branches of a lilac bush and backset; on the other end was a long lean-to stable and gray smoke purled from a smokehouse chimney. A boy, not much younger than himself, was walking across the porch floor on his hands, the unhitched galluses of his denim overalls clicking across the boards. An upside-down pocket was sewn into his pant's leg and stems of black licorice sprang from it.

The hiss of quenching heat blunted the air as the smith again plunged the working end of his pliers into the slack tub. The boy walking on his hands stepped aside for Robey as he mounted the porch and then followed him inside. In the air was the rank sweetness of molasses and coffee, cured bacons and ham.

Old Morphew looked up from his ledger book as the door slapped shut but made no gesture of greeting. He was so much older than Robey remembered since last he had seen him, his chest now gaunt and his body cadaverous. His stertorous breathing came husky and tubercular. They held each other's gaze.

"Mister Morphew," he said, and in the spoken name of the man was his question to the man: Do you remember me? Do you know who I am?

Morphew let go his grasp of the plank table and made up his pipe with tobacco. For the pain of bursitis in his shoulder he lifted his arm over his head and stretched it out and then let it back down. Inside the mercantile the smith's pinging hammer was only a pitched ticktack sound.

"Get'cha some crackers and set down in that cane-bottom, soft-back chair," Morphew said. He pointed to the cracker barrel with his pipe stem and then took a tin can and drew molasses from a black spigot bunged into a cask. Beneath the cask the wooden floor was puddled with a wide black stain where the spigot leaked.

He took the offered can and dipped a cracker. He was hungry and his stomach had begun to gnaw. He ate another, but the gnaw would not be satisfied. While he ate, Morphew studied him from behind his ledger, and when he caught his eye Robey told him what he knew and what he was sent to do and asked where he might go to find the best fighting.

"I know that's where my father will be," he said.

"I ain't heard about Thomas Jackson dead," old Morphew said, pulling on his chin. "Thomas Jackson being dead is hard to imagine. I don't know if I can feature that."

"Ma says he's dead."

"Your mother would know such a thing. She has the gift," Morphew said. "Though I will say one thing to that."

"What's that?"

"Prophesying the death of a man at war seems a safe-enough adventure."

Morphew nodded toward the cracker barrel that he should fill his fist again, then told him what he had heard of the fighting but warned the news was a week old and even if it wasn't it was unreliable at best. He hooked his finger into the spigot and licked them clean.

"Where would I go to find the army?"

"Which army?"

"How many are there?" he asked. He felt his growing tiredness in the warm sweet room. He'd not slept the entire night and understood the ache in his belly to be as much of weariness as hunger. He settled more deeply into the soft-back chair, feeling as if heavy weights had been hung from his limbs.

"There's a lot of them," Morphew was saying. "Last I heard they were in the valley and then they were on the Rappahannock. There's a pile of newspapers there by your feet. You could read up on it, but I wouldn't trust 'em. It's news what's all thirdhand and second best, if you ask me."

"My mother told me to travel south and east to the valley and then down the valley."

"Far be it for me to contradict your mother, but that won't put you on the Rappahannock."

"Where's the Rappahannock at?" He could hear himself speaking the words. The river made sense to him. His father told him to always defend a river on the far bank rather than the near bank and if the near bank was to be defended then do it behind it rather than at the water's edge.

"You go east," Morphew said, and pointed in the direction of east with his pipe stem with such precision that Robey thought east must be a place just outside the wall of the mercantile. That's not so far, he thought.

"Ma told him she'd whip him and hate him forever if he went to war, but he went anyways."

"You can't pound out of the bone what's in the blood," Morphew said.

"He said it was in in my blood too."

"Yessir, he's the travelinist man I ever knew."

"You know you orta whittle a new bung for that molasses cask," Robey said after a lull in the conversation, but already his brain felt thick with tiredness and collapse.

He did not know how long he slept in the soft-back chair. It was a short dreamless sleep that concluded as quickly as it had begun. He could hear the ticktack of the hammer and smell the sweetness. The boy was staring at him upside down, his legs bent at the knees and thrown behind him.

Old Morphew was still at his ledger book holding himself erect on his stiff arms. Again he said Morphew's name as if he had just arrived.

"You ain't running away to fight, are you?" Morphew said sternly.

"No sir," he said, and he was beset with an urgency to get on his way. It was clear to him he never should have stopped. So early in his journey and already he'd conspired to delay himself at the mercantile. It was not his prerogative to doubt his mother's advice, was not his to question or confirm the recondite principles of her clairvoyance.

"You wouldn't lie to me?" Morphew demanded.

"I don't lie."

"No, I don't suppose you do." He pushed a pouch of smoking tobacco across his ledger. "Take this here for your father. He'll want it sure enough, and this too," he said, and pushed forward another pouch full of coffee beans. "He can settle up when he gets back."

"I will be leaving now," Robey said, and stood. "I have a long ways to go and I am anxious to get back soon."

"Good luck," Morphew told him and, stump-legged, followed him onto the porch, with the upside down boy tagging along. The sun had lifted from the horizon and held at a quarter in the sky—he'd slept that long. The cobby horse was lathered and woebegone, her head hanging on her neck. Parked beside the road was a work-sprained ox cart and the teamster carrying a bucket of water to the team. Roped inside the bed of the cart was a nailed coffin made of undressed white-bleached poplar.

"Who you got there?" Morphew yelled out from under the porch roof.

"Mister Skagg's boy," the teamster said, after he located the voice calling him.

"He used to live around here," Robey said.

"Wal', he don't no more," Morphew said.

They watched the teamster deliver another bucket to the thirsty oxen. He wore a black felt hat, a bright red shirt, and trousers ragged at his ankles. His unlined skin was the color of coffee.

"Where you bound from?" Morphew yelled.

"We come up from Lynchburg. Mister Skagg's boy died in hospital there and I am to bring him home."

"How'd he die?"

The teamster dragged his felt hat from his head and held it to his breast. He rubbed at his head trying to figure an answer.

"I just don't know, sir. He was asleep when it happened and didn't tell."

"Damned old fool," Morphew muttered, and then turned his attention to Robey. "It looks to me like you got to the bottom of that horse. How you gonna get where you're going on that ride?"

"I'll just have to walk when the time comes," he said, experiencing an awful sinking of the heart. One look at the cobby horse and he knew that time had come indeed.

"It's a long ways from here and it looks to me like the time is closer than you think. Maybe I can fix you up."

He looked to the teamster and then to the smith down the road at his forge and gestured that Robey should follow him. Behind the mercantile in the lean-to stable, a horse could be heard thrumming through its nose and stamping the wall. Morphew entered the shadowed light of the lean-to and when he returned he was leading the horse forward. It was coal black, stood sixteen hands, and it was clear to see the animal suffered no lack of self-possession.

"That is an oncommon horse," Robey said, unable to help himself in his admiration.

"He's a warm blood," Morphew said, "and I will tell you one thing. When he goes, he goes some bold."

"Who does he belong to?"

"The man who rode him in here died in that cane-bottom soft-back chair not a week ago and I buried him in the cemetery. That's to say the horse's ownership is in limbo but in my possession, so you can say he's mine right now."

"I have never seen a horse like that."

"The German says he's a Hanovarian. He's a fine horse,

with an equable disposition, but I'll warn you, he don't much like other horses."

"Which side were he on?"

"The man or the horse?"

"It don't much matter, does it?"

"Not if you're dead now, does it?"

From the darkness of the stable's interior, Morphew fetched a bridle, blanket, and saddle with holsters draping the pommel. He then fished into the black space where the rafters crossed the beam.

"You know what these are?"

"Yes sir."

"What are they?"

"Army Colts."

"Of course you do. They are .44 Army Colts. Do you know how to use them?"

"Yes sir."

"Show me how."

Robey cradled one of the the revolvers in his hands, hefting its weight and sighting along the length of its barrel. He deftly knocked out the pin and removed the cylinder and then looked to Morphew who produced a box of cartridges, percussion caps, and grease. Robey tore the covering from one of the cartridges and poured the powder into the chamber and then seated the bullet. After he loaded the cylinders he greased the head of each bullet. He then set a brass cap at the rear of each chamber. Then he repeated the process with the second revolver.

"Take them," Morphew said. "The horse and the pistols."

"I can't do that," he said. "Ma said I warn't to ask for no help."

Morphew thrust out his lower lip and scrutinized him before he spoke and when he finally did he began in anger and
with impatience.

"Talking like that tells me you ain't got half sense to be out
here doing what you're doing."

Morphew's breathing caught in his throat and he had to
draw down into his lungs to find it again. His face reddened
and his words became dull mutterings as water slid from his
right eye. A pain passed through him taking the color from
his cheeks. When he spoke again his throat was constricted
and his words were as if winnowed in his throat channel.

"I respect your mother. She is an uncommon woman
among women, but you just can't go boggling around the
countryside. Things out there ain't like they used to be."

"How's that?"

"You used to be able to trust people."

In old Morphew's urgent composition were unspoken words:
But I still trust you.

"You saddle and bridle this horse and you meet me out
front. I will write you a paper saying this horse is mine, which
by rights it is, and that currently it is in your custody."

Morphew turned his back and stumped over the worn
ground, making the short distance between the stable and
the mercantile.

He was alone with the horse and as he studied it, he understood the horse to be making decisions about him as well.
He'd not known such a horse as this had ever been made and
could not help but feel inferior to the animal. He was a young
stallion and through his body he was deep and big set. His
head was light in build and his eyes were large. His neck was

long and fine and his tail set high, but his shoulders were built massive. His muscles were dense and ran strong and wide in the loin. His legs were short in the cannon bones but his joints supple, strong, and substantial. His hoofs were high in front, behind and below, and the frog carried well off the ground.

He stepped forward and touched his hands to its long face. The coal black horse let his stroke to its cheek, neck, and muzzle. He then stroked its back and shoulders and worked his way down each leg, increasing the strength of his touch on the wide forearms and gaskins. He caught the horse's eyes with his own and the horse seemed inclined to tolerate him, if not be actually fond of him. After working his hands firmly over the animal's body, he bridled the coal black horse and set the blanket. He cinched the rig, and after telling the horse what he was going to do he caught the stirrup, swung up, and settled in the saddle. He then told the horse he was ready and the horse was willing.

When he rode around front, old Morphew was sitting in a rocker he'd dragged onto the porch. The upside-down boy was playing his hands as close to the rockers as he could without pinching his fingers. Morphew had a gunnysack for him with cans of deviled ham, pork and beans, and condensed milk. He pulled himself erect and labored his body from the porch.

"Don't get cocky riding that horse," he said as he adjusted the stirrup leathers. "A man rides a horse like that he begins to think he's above every other man."

Old Morphew then stepped back from the horse's side. Youthfulness twinkled inside him. He enjoyed the businessman's satisfaction of a completed transaction well done. It was in seeing his pleasure that Robey determined the old man must have experienced a recent great terror inside his heart cage or the depths of his mind and only now, frightened and wounded, was returning to himself.

"Rupert," Morphew yelled over to the German, "how is it you're not drunk today?"

Without pausing in his work, the bent man thrust the middle finger of his right hand over his head. Morphew laughed at this—a mischievous little game they played.

"Hunchbacks are often smarter than we are," he said, as if it were a truth underappreciated.

"Don't that boy ever stand up?" Robey said.

"No," Morphew said, casting a glance at the boy walking on his hands. "As a matter of fact he don't. He is an upside-down boy. Bet you've never heard or seen one of them."

"No sir. I don't believe I have."

"Well, you are in for an education and I just hope you live long enough to tell about it."

"I will."

"That's right. You find your father," he said, waving him away, "and you bring him home and we'll settle up."

With that, he rode off on the coal black horse with the heavy revolvers in the holsters at his thighs. As he disappeared from sight, Morphew noticed the German had wandered to his porch and was suddenly standing at his side. The German marveled on the beauty of the horse's flowing movement, its grace in stride, and he commented with small wonder on the horse's affinity for the boy.

"It's a horse that leaves quite an impression," Morphew said.

"It is the kind of horse that can get you killed."

"I thought about that."

"And what did you think when you thought about that?"

"I thought a lot of things. I thought about his mother. I thought about how he's his father's son and he is a-goin' either way he can. I thought how gettin' in trouble ain't hard, but gettin' out of it is."

"I thought you'd think how where he's going the horse might be smarter than him."

"I thought that too."

3

It was beautiful to ride the back of the coal black horse and in those first days of journey they traveled constantly. The valley when he discovered it was luxuriant with grass and clover. The red-clay roads were wide and hard packed and the road cuts were dry and banked.

As the days drew by they passed silently through fields, swamps, pastures and orchards. They rode through marsh where the water table was only a few spades deep, but the corduroyed lanes of passage were high set and well staked. They crossed acres of fresh turned earth, plowed straight and harrowed and sown with wheat, rye, and oats shooting the surface and knitting it green. They encountered walls of pine so thick it took days to skirt to find a throughway and when they did it was through a land of wind-thrown trees, or dead on the stump, the crooked and angled limbs bleached white with sun.

In his urgency, sleep was Robey's bane and he tried with all his might to stay awake days at a time, but finally he relented and learned to fall asleep on the back of the coal black horse as it seemed to share the same mind with him in the direction it maintained. From then on, when he grew tired, he merely pulled a blanket over his head and dropped his chin upon his rocking breast and slept and the horse would sleep too, walking on in its repose, covering a length of four miles every hour, its hooves invisible for the dust and gauze of heat, or veiled by lightning on the black path as the flashes directed their way in the electric, combusting, and starless night.

Whole days and whole nights went by; how many he lost track of and could not tell. He'd not known there was so much country beyond the hollows and so flat and undulating and the deep-running streambeds, the dense thickets of wild rose, the sudden, vertical-walled mountains. Although with his own eyes he had seen the vast distances to be witnessed skimming across the mountaintops, he'd not seen so far inside the land, not seen such verdant meadows and lush pasturage and the great built houses he saw, ever in his life before.

In moments he thought he'd have seen the ocean by now, or the majestic cities his father talked about. He thought he would have crossed shiny iron rails or entered the funnels of tree-lined boulevards terminating in the grand squares where government and business did their work. His father had told him of how broad and limitless the world, how close the woods, how endless the tidy green forest, how steep the climbs and sharp were the switchbacks' rocky descents. Out west, his father had told him, nature's work was as yet undone. The rivers still sought their beds and in their seeking they swelled to measureless proportions and were as if vast inland seas appearing and disappearing. The mountains were high and tumbled and rose to invisibility. There was desert land and canyon land. There were trees so wide at the stump they were impossible to chop down and in some places there were no trees at all as far as the eye could see. The weather was big beyond the Mississippi and angry and lasted for weeks. The cold was too cold, the hot was too hot, the water was too much or none at all. Nature was laid bare naked: sparkling sand, wind-scored stone, leeching mineral, hanging and split rock dividing the buffeting wind. Wetness sought dryness and the wind the tallest trees to strike down and the lightning the flattest land. Out west was the mine, the quarry, the nursery, the smithy of a maker.

At first he collected what he could of food and weapons and there was plenty to be found and picked over. But then he stopped his hoarding and rode on with only a blanket, oilcloth, loaded pistols, a knife, and a canteen and managed to find a handful of parched corn, or buttermilk, ginger snaps, a sack of navy beans whenever he needed to satisfy his hunger and often there was to be found in the ruins of the army's plumbeous-colored wagons such odd fare as sardines, pickled lobster, canned peaches, and coffee. He thought he'd starve before he'd steal, but that was before he was faced with starving.

As the days went by, he began to attend the smells of frying bacon and stalk the cow paths spattered with fresh dung. When necessary, he filched field corn from the cribs or caught stray chickens, a cooling pie, a ham hung in a smokehouse, and when there was none of this to be found he ate berries, ramps, and wild garlic. He ate watercress and drank tea he boiled from acorns.

He left the valley in an easterly direction and he crossed again where mountaintops were wreathed by terrible winds, where mountains were heaped on mountains whose cloud-capped summits seemed to call him and he thought someday he'd like to return to them and search through their aerie mists to stand on their peaks.

There were also beautiful and isolate moments in his searching days. He followed deer paths into their notched parks where thirty or fifty head grazed like cattle. He saw pools of water where there were so many fish they climbed on each others' backs, sparkling in the sunlight, to tongue the hatch. Down lanes he traveled there were estates, brightly lit against the night's darkness and untouched by war or the news of war. He saw tiny villages set in mountain glens, pretty farms and houses whose existence was pristine and without evidence of what was overcome to be so pure.

One night in the twilight world of an early evening, he heard organ music playing in the trees and could smell the heavy scents of burst pine pollen. Somewhere there were people gathered and they were worshipping and their choral voices hymned in the darkness. His mother had beliefs, but his father was a freethinker and was fond of saying that with soap, baptism could be a good thing. He suspected that his beliefs fell somewhere in the middle between his mother and father. Curious as to the music's source, he suggested the horse in its direction and anticipated arriving at its source, but it ebbed and then disappeared as mysteriously as it had occurred and he wondered, What could it have been?

He continued on until he found wedged in a declivity of stone a standing horse that'd hung itself up a long time ago. It was made of white bones whose ribs grew moss and legs sustained runner vines and the bone of its skull was a garland of white-flowered creepers. The horse must have plunged through and broke itself and become trapped and could not escape, and now when the wind was right it sounded music in those bones.

HIS FACE ALTERNATELY wind galled and sunburned and his limbs numb with cold and listless with heat, he had descended into the vast green northeasterly valley, crossed the upheaved blue mountains, and descended once again onto the piney plain, where the air quaked and trembled as it endured its own heated weight. His mother had told him to continue up the valley, but by all other accounts it was to the east where the army was to be found.

By now he was joined as one with the horse. His thighs and legs were soaked with its lather, his clothes stained through with its sweat. So too his hands and where he rubbed his face and finger-combed his hair, and he could not imagine ever parting with the jewel of it. The horse held possession of both his waking and sleeping mind. He dreamt of the horse and in each sleep the horse multiplied until they became so many horses he could not keep count of them. The coal black horses were the first horses and the only horses ever to have been. They were not horses, but like something of the other—the man-eaters: the lion or wolf or bear, or man himself. Only they were more true, more noble of birth, more singular of purpose and intent. When they ran, they ran in a glorious periphery of whiteness that disappeared the earth beneath them and the air above the earth to the spring of their ribs. There were no legs on boy or horse. He was blank from the knees and the effect was that of riding light, as if light were spindrift and he was borne in its froth and was swept along on the horse he rode: the winged horse, the born horse, the horse out of the blood, the horse pulling the light of day across the sky.

He thought to tell the horse of these events visiting his mind in dream, but could not bring himself to do so for how weak and lovesick they left him. Every time he tried he felt as if he would collapse to the ground. He thought if he were to tell he would lose what little there was left of him. To tell what he believed the horse already knew would be to lose himself forever in the horse.

It was during this time that he resolved he would keep the horse and by whatever means possible he would pay Morphew the price of its purchase and he would find the heirs to the dead cavalryman who owned the horse before Morphew and he would pay again.

HE RODE ON THROUGH the snarled forests of the flat land, rough and bluntly savage, and over sweeps of inexplicably burned and gouged terrain, and it was here one day when he came upon death.

It was long before he arrived at the shattered and blown house, long before he even knew it existed that he was drawn in its direction. Perhaps it was the eerie silence in the place he sensed beyond the tree line. Perhaps it was the emptiness he felt in the atmosphere. He felt a falling-off inside himself and a telling in his mind that he was entering a place of grave dedication. Then there was a flush of vultures and on the shadowed ground movement into light, and a pack of dogs slunk by and with the dogs was carried the unmistakable smell. It was in their jaws and chests and soaked into their shamed faces.

For no apparent reason, men had been killed here, their

souls set astray and their bodies left piled like rotting cord wood in ditches and behind files of sharpened stakes. The men's bones wore tatters of flesh and cloth and where they were piled it was difficult to tell how many men there were. He had no one to guide him through these ghostly regions of horrible event and him with so little understanding of how many people on the earth, in this moment it seemed as if half of them were dead and left unburied. Their smell was like a fresh poison possessing the wind to become the wind. Though he had never smelled the death of men before, he knew the smell as if it were a knowledge born into him.

He dismounted for vague reasons of respect and together with the horse he walked across the battlefield to its border and into the dark woods. When he turned to mount the horse his foot sank into the ground and his ankle became trapped in the rib cage of a single man buried alone in a shallow washed-out grave. The man's bones were chalky and withered and broken and one arm was raised to his gray skull as if in salute and his finger bones were clenched in the fist of a painful death. The man's death must have occurred so long before the others. Had this clearing seen war before? Was this a place where war resided like a natural animal in wait?

He did not know the answers to his questions and did not even care to think about them for very long. He simply knew with all these men dead he must be getting close. He thought with all these men dead fighting war, it must be that war was winning.

AT NIGHT MOST PEOPLE went to bed, but not all. To be encountered on the roads was the sound of pounding hooves and to be avoided were bands of armed men on the backs of their hard-ridden horses. This was easily done, but not so easy to avoid were the lone riders slipping along silently in the dark. He met such riders on the road, men whose violence always seemed to be within them, violence that was convulsive and dangerous. They rode with their reins loose in one hand and with the other they held a carbine or a double-barreled shotgun, upright, with the butt resting on their thigh.

When he could not avoid these encounters he slowed and half-raised an arm in the common gesture of lone riders meeting on back roads. Most often they were as wary as he was and wanted as little to do with him as he wanted with them. They had their own secret fears and reasons to avoid being seen on the roads. They were on their own private missions. But then seeing the coal black horse materialize from the shadows and grow upon approach, they'd swivel in the saddle for the better look and he could feel their eyes on his back.

Then came one late evening when he was riding down a deep-cut bowered lane with a snake-rail fence running along both its sides. The air carried heavy and was too dense to carry much reach of surrounding sound. From ahead there came the profile of a dark rider in relief from a dogleg bending the road. The dark rider paused to consider them and then came on. He grew as he made his approach and when they passed on the lane the dark rider pulled rein and hailed him by a name that was not his own. Fooled by this trick of mistaken identity, he stopped in the road and turned, but the coal black horse did not want to stop and he quickly wised up to its misgiving when he heard the muffled sound made by the rider's thumb drawing back the hammer on the shotgun he carried. His heels raked hard, but it was not necessary. The coal black horse was already driving into a sudden run. The horse broke fast and drove all out for the dogleg ahead and he held as tight as he could because the horse was making for it with a power he did not know it possessed.

Bent to the horse's neck, he clung hard so as not to be un-horsed and still had little hope for when they made the sharp corner. He feared for how fast the ground would rise because he knew he'd not be able to hold on when the horse set left and threw right to make its turn. But rather than drop its shoulder to make the turn, the horse continued to climb in stride and at the last instant made a great winging leap out of the cut and over the high snake-rail fence and into a wall of briars that grew on the other side. His body whipped in the saddle but he clenched up and held with the last he had. In that same moment the shotgun fired, and simultaneously a covey of quail went up in their wake. There was a raucous thrashing as the briars tore at them for some distance until they burst free onto brushy ground and then across a cutting, where they disappeared into a wood on the other side.

But it was not this dangerous encounter that lingered in his mind. Rather, it was the poise and equanimity of the horse that he wondered on, its sense and knowledge of men. After-ward, there would be other episodes, but he did not need to wait to hear the hammer drawn back or to feel the spray of buckshot falling on his shoulders before they were dodging into the next bend in the road. It would happen again and again, but by then he was digging his heels into the horse's sides and it was rising into the bit on big floating steps and they were disappeared.

ANOTHER DAY PASSED and then another and he could feel the urgency of his mother's imperative weighing on his mind and body. He could feel the responsibility of the promise he'd made her. He was to find his father and bring him back to his home where he lived. And he remembered she said he was not to dally along the way but to find his father as soon as he could and to find him by July. But why July? What did she know about July before it even happened? Or had it already happened? He wondered what month it was. Surely it was not yet July.

"Tomorrow," he repeated. Maybe tomorrow would be the day when he would find his father. But then tomorrow came and went and he felt no closer to the river where the army was said to be than he did the day before. He had no idea the land was so big and the many crosses its roads made.

He was now in a hot and wet country ridden with flies and he often wished for flight and to enter the realm where the birds darted and sliced the air. He wished the coal black horse to grow the wings he dreamed and fly him through the air. The wind on the plain east of the valley was long and tangled and he was homesick, fatigued, and disillusioned. His strength was about gone and his limbs felt as if borrowed from a man a hundred years old.

In darkness, he left the road and followed a stitch of path into the trees and then left the path and urged the horse to find a route in the pathless forest. He continued on, desiring distance from the traffic of humans. He wanted a place remote and undisturbed where he could collect himself, where he could lie down and sleep, lest he slide from the horse's back and tumble to the ground. He needed to lie on the earth and rest his thin sore body and renew his thowless spirit.

He unsaddled the coal black horse to let its back cool in the moon-dappled shade. He ran his hands over its legs and lifted each foot to check for cracks in the hoof walls. He sorted the cockleburs from its high-set tail. He wondered at how indifferent the horse was to pain, how immune to weakness. He had long since come to understand and accept how superior the animal was to him, and he did not mind this fact but appreciated it.

"You are tough as a old ox," he said, briefly catching an eye's lateral vision with his own.

He shook out the sweat-stained saddle blanket and lay down in front of the horse on a bed of green ferns and where arched fiddleheads unfolded and a lead tied loosely to his wrist.

He looked up into the horse's face and told the animal to be patient with him, that he was still a boy and that he should sleep awhile before they moved on. He did not want to slip off and break his neck in the dirt.

"I am tired," he said as if tiredness were a thing of longing. The horse responded by nosing his chest and blowing gently against his face.

"I am dirty as a pig," he said in agreement. The horse lifted a foot and set it down heavy. It grunted and then found bunches of grass at his side to enfold with its lips and tear free. Its head shot up as it chewed and it glanced to the rear.

You eat a little bit, he thought. Just a bit of sleep for me and we'll be on our way.

But it was a troubled sleep waiting for him. That day on the road he'd seen something his mind would not let go of. It was not that they were men alive or dead. It was not that they were men torn or ravaged or made horrible. Then his mind did let go and his eyes closed and his breathing steadied and he listened to the horse cropping again and chewing what it'd found, its eyes, its ears, its nose always ready for reasons to fly.

WHEN HE AWOKE, he was refreshed. He sat up and swept the May bugs from his face and hair. He stood in light and when he did he learned that beyond the small clearing and its edge of woods where he'd slept was a bow made by a flat river where swallows danced lightly on streams of air. The sunlight was clear and strong and he could see the river's glaring sparkle without seeing the water's surface. He led the horse in its direction where he found another green and there he tied the horse to a lead where it could browse the fresh grass.

He proceeded on to the riverbank, wading through deep ferns and a flowering thicket, a hand held in front of his eyes for how bright the sun glare reflecting off the riffles. He stepped forward and then he sat down and let himself slide the bank on his backside to dangle his feet from the edge of the bluff overlooking where the broad flat river looped. His father told him rivers were difficult to defend. They created meanders and meanders needed to be closed and in doing so they tended to suck up troops.

The bluff was littered with softened pine needles and the water under the sun was the color of caramel. He thought to dangle his legs in the water, but it ran too far beneath the rim of the bluff. His father said rivers break lines of sight and impede lateral movements. It was rivers where possibilities began and ended.

He sat for a long time, resting on a bed of pine needles in the cool shade. He knew he needed to be on his way and soon

enough he would mount the coal black horse and follow east
into the sun. Behind him he could hear the horse snuffing
and tearing grass. He realized he'd not eaten in several days
and needed food as well as he needed travel. Lately the byways had been clogged with the traffic of refugees, mule driv-
ers cursing, men teaming haggard draft horses, high-piled
wagons teetering with trunks, home goods, and furniture.
There were women with green hides sewn to their feet who
drove cows and pigs before them and there were barefoot boys
and girls cutting the air with switches behind flocks of im-
perious geese and waddling ducks who griped like spoiled
children. He saw a lone man shabbily dressed with a kid goat
slung over his shoulders, a little boy carrying a rabbit by its ears.
They pushed wheelbarrows and pulled handcarts that were
laden with carpet sacks, churns, hand tools. For the most they
were poor and motely. Their bodies were thin and drawn in
stark contrast to the fattening food stock—the beeves, hogs,
and milch cows that were leading them south and west.

And there were the lone teamsters with their cargo of the
maimed and dead. He wondered if they were the same driv-
ers he'd seen in the far distance from the high place above
the Twelve Mile, old men with their rude wagons and broken horses hauling the casualties of war back to their homes,
only to return again for another load of the torn and shattered. Sometimes there was a box and other times there was
tightly bound swaddling in the shape of a man. Some men
waved to him and others just stared as if he were the strange
one who'd crossed by accident into the land of limbless men.
Maybe these teamsters were but a few in number, the desig-
nated, and this was their mission, their destiny—freighting

the damaged from the sundered world. Two days ago it was a black phaeton with glass sides pulled by a matched pair of carriage horses. It didn't matter, the old man at the footboard holding the reins and whip, the box inside the glass walls, it was still the same.

There were other travelers also to be seen on the roads and byways and on first occurrence he did not completely understand who these strange bands of men and women were, and these his mind could not let go of. It seemed common enough to him that he should see black men wearing checkered homespun and walking behind the horses the white men rode and not so unusual that the black men themselves would sometimes be riding. But he'd not seen before in his life a black man with a leather strap collaring his neck and being led down the road by a chain. His quickest thought was that the man was a criminal, but in the next instant he knew better.

These encounters, they increased in number and frequency until yesterday. He did not know what told the horse there was a strangeness approaching from the north, but it stopped and raised its head and directed its ears forward. He pressed with his left thigh and clucked in his throat and they stepped off the road and into the tree shade and waited. He was not so intent on hiding as he was avoiding being seen by the silent, alien caravan that was approaching, for advancing on him was no jingle of harness, no rattle of a bridle, no cough, no muffled tramp of feet or plodding hooves. There was no gabble of voices or creaking wheel axles, not even the silent approach of the lone rider he'd learned to detect in the extension of his mind. There was not a sound or feeling he could name, but an eeriness. It was as strange as the birth of an unnatural—the oncoming surround of utter silence they carried with them as they moved down the road, as if a troupe escaped from hell, seemingly without motion and heated and on the edge of burning.

When the vanguard hove into view they were the roughest men he'd ever seen. They rode all manner of horse and rig. They rode gaunt horses with pinch-nosed hackamoors that wrung their tails alongside warm-bloods wearing blinker hoods and four-reined bridles. There were wild and bony horses snubbed short that didn't so much walk as they skittered and pawed across the ground sideways the way an insect does. Some of these men were shirtless and rode without blankets or saddles. Their faces were painted and their long hair knotted with leather. He wondered on the vanity in these men as some wore feather plumes in the bands of their slouch hats and red and paisley kerchiefs at their necks. Others wore ropes of shells around their necks and their heads were made up with blue and vermillion. There was also a black man, face tattooed and wearing a beaver hat, who rode among them, the silvered butt of a short-barreled muskatoon bouncing on his thigh.

Following behind were runaway slaves that'd been rounded up and formed into coffles and marched back south. When the chains had run out they'd been yoked with forked branches cut from trees and lashed at their necks. They were a silent dusty procession and fantastic in appearance. Their clothes were often a flannel patchwork, or torn calicoes or canvas cloth, or cut-up blankets sewn into smocks and trousers suspended at the waist. They wore coverlets gashed in the center, dropped over their heads, and closed round them with a belt. The children were dressed in overshirts with no underclothes beneath them. While most wore rags and castoffs, a few were better dressed than the riders. One chained man wore a smart black suit and a low-topped bowler hat.

Bringing up the rear was another knot of the manhunters and a two-wheeled dog car with penned and slobbering hounds riding beneath the driver's high seat. The dogs looked his way with their drawn red eyes but didn't make a sound. They were dogs trained to hunt what they hunted without a care for anything else, and their chained and yoked quarry walked the road before them.

After that, he wanted distance from human beings and the roads they traveled. He wanted the ancient overgrown animal paths found in deep and trackless country. He wanted the parallel roads traveled by the drovers and the livestock, the poor, the runaways themselves.

4

THERE WAS A RARE SETTLING accomplished by a silent concert of light, air, and water. His still-tired mind lulled into repose where it stayed for a time until disrupted by a thrashing in the leaf mold beneath the brush. He smiled at how a foraging squirrel could make more of a racket than a mast-rooting hog. He knew he had to be on his way and, this morning, ached with the guilt of recalcitrance. He wanted his days back. Wanted time to be his again. He idly tossed a stick in the direction of the racket. There was a long silence and then a scraping sound and then from a branch high over his head the squirrel began to chatter, scolding him for throwing the stick in its direction, scolding him for his presence on the cutbank.

The sun soon shifted in the sky and found the patch of ground where he sat and he was blotted with light. He thought what sport it would be to fish this river. From the hard-twigged bushes came the chit notes of songbirds. Swallows were diving for the riverbank below his feet, building their nests. In the tops was a breeze combing the spiring trees and then it was quiet again as if a hand suddenly raised had been let down. Behind him he could hear the horse tearing away tussocks of grass.

He tried to recall having slept the night through but could not.

On the far bank emerged the figure of a human, a bent little woman. A cob pipe protruded from the shaded confines of her bonnet. A length of braided hair extended down her back. She carried a wooden bucket and a cane fish pole rocked on her shoulder, no more than a harmless curiosity. She stepped down from the grassy mull bank to the stony shore, the toes of her shoes poking from beneath her gingham skirts.

He thought to slide away into the woods, but following her was a gaggle of squat white geese and this was walking food. A duck was selling for twenty-five cents and a goose was fifty cents or about that.

He watched as she studied the water downstream and then wandered back upstream along the stone-cobbled shore. The geese followed her in both directions, bumping into each other as they toddled to turn and catch up. He didn't have any coins. Maybe she'd take trade, but what to trade? He could steal just one, but in his thieving to date he'd never stole from anyone he'd seen to be an owner.

The little old woman did not seem intent on fishing and after a while she dropped the fishing pole, sat down on her bucket, and concentrated on smoking her pipe. The geese wandered about in idleness and mild confusion until the little woman spat. They gathered on the spot, bumping into each other, inspecting her phlegm for some time. Then a goose found a grub and drew the attention of the others and they gathered there next. The woman continued to enjoy her pipe, sending a steady succession of gray puffs into the air. Over the pines, crows in flight made their raucous calls. Their sound came on suddenly like a snapping bough. A mobbed owl hove into view and crossed his vision over the river's surface. The owl slid low, found the dark understory on the near bank, and disappeared. The crows, having never shown themselves, broke off their pursuit.

It was then he noticed the lazy water browning in color and beginning to rise. At first it was slow and he did not know if it was happening at all, so slow was its beginning, but then it rose more rapidly. The current quickened and there came wreaths of feather-white foam swirled about the edges of vortexes that made ripping sounds as they sucked shut. Stems and leafy branches followed and then a broad limb of dried wood.

Upstream, there must have been a powerful rain as the river continued to swell until it had become a black muddy wash. The little woman stood, took her bucket in hand, and walked backward as the water followed her, nagging at her feet with every step she made. The geese assembled on her steps, flustered and squanking in confusion. She stepped cautiously and he wanted to yell that she should run. Then she did. She turned into a trot that took her to higher ground where the sand and gravel was closed over by hummocks of grass sewn into the red earth. She jumped the grassy step, the flustered geese climbing behind her, and watched as the river gently heaved and cuffed its high-water mark.

It occurred to him, as it continued its rising, that it just might not stop, so fast and powerful was it coming on. He left off his concern for the little woman and began to scamper backward on his palms and heels. But this was not quick enough, so he stood to run, and it was in that moment of standing that a great chunk of earth the river had slowly been carving began to subside. The bank gave way beneath his feet and he was being let down into the caramel water on a slab of red dirt collapsing into the river.

His descent was slow and inexorable, and however hard he strained to scuttle the falling bank he could not keep himself from being shrugged away. He went under the dirty surface and even as he pushed the bottom to rise for air the deluge was already receding, and when he stood he found himself standing waist deep in muddy water. His wetted body cooled and yet was heated as if hornet-stung in the sluggish frothy water. His clothes skimmed with a slick of red clay and sluiced from his fingertips as if milk or blood.

"Yo, boy," a voice called out. It was the little woman with the cane fish pole coming down to the water's edge from the dry bank. Other than her nose and the bowl of her pipe, her face was shrouded in bonnet. "You drownded yourself?" she inquired.

He cleared his burning nostrils and spit. He dragged himself into the shallows and pawed his way through the flooded briars, his shoes slogging through the scum until he reached a hard bed of silt and stone. He pawed at his face and eyes again. He shook out his arms, shucking their wetness into the air.

The little woman was laughing at his calamity. She was a strange and ugly woman with narrow shoulders and a long beakish nose that ran constantly. Just as she'd wipe at it, another drip would form. About her being was the rank smell of old sweat that surpassed even the stagnant earth of the riverbank. With her geese jostling to flank her at the water's edge that they might stare at him too, he thought she also made quite the comical.

"Don't you look a picture," she cackled. "You have got to be careful. Accidents happen out here."

"Is this the Rappahannock?" he asked as he climbed the bank to stand at her feet. Hers was not a very kind face. Her face actually made him dizzy to look at as her skin seemed to run in the sunlight with a swarming fluidlike vibration. His body iced as he realized that she was crawling with lice. They were running her skin in streaming volutions that swirled her cheeks and forehead and across her lips and yet she did not seem to notice.

"This little trickle?" she said. "Don't be a ignoramus." And then she said, "What do you want with the Rappahannock?"

"You ain't a woman," he said, before he could stop his voice in his throat. "You're a man."

"Every beggar's got his stick for beating off the dogs," the little woman said.

She then swiped the bonnet and braided hair from her head in a single motion and she was indeed a man. The little man then unbuttoned the dress and shed it from his shoulders. Without the dress he was a queer, spindly little man, built like a boy with a boy's frame and a boy's muscles, but in the light his face skin revealed to run evermore with the motion of vibrating water. His bare neck and the wisps of hairs at his collar were beset. His naked arms and the backs of his hands were likewise a struggling infestation, but beyond belief he seemed to pay it no mind. Still, there appeared nothing to fear from him except his infestation.

"You really never know a man's true nature." The little man laughed.

His face held an expression behind which little could be seen for the crawling mask he wore. The little man rooted in his ear with his finger, as if there could possibly be something that would irritate him, and then looked at it.

His voice turned to sharp rule and still looking at his finger he said, "You intend to jine up, or what?"

Robey shook his head. His stomach had become a turning of knots. He could not look at the man's crawling skin and he could not look away from it for how mesmerizing. He was not afraid, but he felt better when he knew where the little man's face was, the same way he wanted to know where a disappeared snake crawled to when he came across one in the forest.

"No," he said.

"I were in the army for a time," the little man said wistfully. "I spent my days in the mud marching through wet cornfields. I was trod on and ridden over by every big-mouthed son of a bitch who had a horse. I'll be hanged if I know anything more about the matter than that." Then he paused and said, "I couldn't wait to get back home."

The little man was funny to him and he began to take pity on him for how lost in the world a man so little as him must be when all other men were so big.

"Food?" the little man said.

"Lately I been kind of off it," Robey said.

"Hungry then, ain't ya'."

"I been feelin' like a walking belly," he said.

"You afoot?"

He told him he wasn't and asked that he should wait while he forded the river to retrieve his horse and kit. The little man agreed to this and Robey slogged through the water to make the far bank. The horse was waiting where he'd left it but was contrary this morning and had little intention of crossing. He patiently saddled the animal and slung his haversack over the pommel. He jammed a pistol in his belt and then coaxed the horse to the riverbank, but again it shied when at the water's edge and kicked that it should not get wet. He stopped to stroke the animal's eyes and soft muzzle.

"Can you handle it?" the little man yelled across through his cupped hands.

He spoke to the horse how they'd feed and water and get on their way, and only with the utmost of patience was he able to convince the horse across the river.

"Boy, I like the looks of that horse," the little man said when they came up from the river.

"He's a good horse," Robey said.

"I had me a good saddle horse I was riding," the little man said. But by then he was back in the branches and was striking a path in the woods with the white geese waddling along behind him.

Robey followed the little man and the geese to his house where the window glass was broken and from inside there were more geese stretching their long necks and staring out from the jagged openings. Or they tottled on the wide veranda, curious and birdy about events they found significant, yet were invisible to the human eye. The little man told him to stay put and not to move while he fetched them food to eat, and he was to refrain from using the well as the well house was charred over from fire and still stank of wet smoke and its water was rancid.

The little man disappeared inside the house and it wasn't long before he came out carrying an immense platter heaped with half-warmed sauerkraut, fried onions, salt pork, and cold beef. In his other hand he held a coffeepot. He squatted in the yard as he set the platter on the ground between them and after taking up a handful of kraut and a slab of beef, he urged Robey that he should also take some food and eat. He was so hungry he did not pause to reach into the plate after the little man.

They ate in silence, gorging their food and grunting the way dogs do. For Robey it was because he was so hungry, but for the little man it seemed to be the way he knew how to eat. Between mouthfuls the little man began telling Robey the long story of how he'd just come home from the war on furlough, the hounds of hell on his ass all the way, only to find that raiders and renegades had been at his house. When he told of their destructiveness his swarming eyelids quivered and his hooded eyes blanked with hatred.

"There is no sign of my family and I can only hope they are safe," he said. But there was no hope in his voice, his affect flat and melancholy.

"You're going to look for them," Robey said, sympathetic to the little man's plight.

"Why yes I am," he said. "Thank you."

The little man patted his full belly and belched and insisted Robey do the same and when he did the little man thought that hilarious. He slapped his thighs and insisted they do it again. Then they reclined in the grass and while rolling a cigarette, the little man told Robey that war had its other sides too.

"In war," he said, "the best bad things are often obtain-able," and then he offered him the coffeepot, but when Robey thumbed the hinged lid it smelled of whiskey inside and he declined.

"Oh, go ahead," the little man said. "Have you a little shot in the neck. It won't hurt you none. They's a twenty-gallon demijohn settin' right inside the door."

The little man took a long gulping drink as if to prove how abundant the amount of whiskey.

Robey thought how the little man must have had a rough go of it, being little and all and then to come home and find what he'd worked for wrecked and vandalized and his family missing and maybe dead. But now he was wary for the changes in the little man. Within short time of his whiskey-drinking, something had come over him, or had risen up from inside him. Either way he was being overtaken and it was coming on fast.

He told the little man whiskey was nothing he'd ever drunk before and at the moment it just didn't interest him, but he was grateful for the food and thought he should consider being on his way.

The little man laughed, as if satisfied with the logic of his answer, but it was an ill-tempered laugh. He continued to drink and then he tried again to interest Robey in joining him, but he declined.

"But it ain't no fun drinking alone," the little man said, as if an appeal remembered, one made to him by another somewhere in his past.

"No," Robey said again. "I don't want any whiskey, thank you."

"But it's good whiskey. It slows time," the little man said, his voice sweet and wheedling. He told him it made all your cares a will-o'-the-wisp. He drank off another full draft and then another until he was swirling his finger inside the empty pot to catch the dregs.

"It's time I was going," Robey said again and he felt a flush of anger for how foolish he'd been and a sudden unreasoned fear came over him. He was now ensnared by the little man and he'd allowed it to happen.

"Before you go, sell me that horse," the little man suggested, licking his fingers. "So's I can ride it to search for my family."

"It ain't mine to sell," Robey said, fighting to quell the apprehension in his voice. He knew he could no longer be timid, no longer hesitant and compliant. He didn't know who this man was, but he knew this man's mind was set and he would never give up the idea of possessing the horse.

"You stole it," the man said, and when he suddenly stood Robey pulled himself from the ground to also stand.

"It was lent me," he said.

"You love that horse, don't ya'?"

Robey did not reply. His hand went to his waist where the butt of his pistol hung in his belt.

"What every horse lover don't understand is that every horse is someday gonna die," the little man said. Inside his swirling complexion his eyes had reddened. His voice was shrill as a child's.

"There is other horses in the world, I'll grant you that," Robey said.

"Sell it to me and tell your man it were killed."

"I can't do that."

"I say nobody lets out a horse like that."

"Mister Morphew let me that horse. I have a paper to prove it." His face burned at the charge, that his honesty should be questioned and that he should stoop to defend himself.

He also knew it made no difference to the little man that he should have such a paper to prove his word.

"I could kill that horse," the little man said, and drew the revolver he wore in his belt and aimed at the coal black horse. Robey knew it was true and he knew the only witness would be the wind and the trees. "Give to me that horse or I will blow the top of its head off."

Later, he remembered feeling a numbing shock to his skull and remembered singling out the shot that fired from the gun and then seeing in the rail of his vision the little man holding the gun. He knew he shook his head in disbelief when the revolver turned on him and at the same time knew his own hand held a revolver and that he fired his weapon into the dirt at his feet and then his brain convulsed. His mind split open and without there being a sense of light, there was an eclipse of light and then there was only a throbbing blackness and then there was only blackness.

When he finally came to consciousness it was in night's darkness and the sky was lit with stars. He did not fully understand what had happened to him but understood there was nothing he could do. Days may have passed, but he could not tell because he had no idea of time. Neither did he have an idea of place—the sky above, the earth below. His head felt broken and seemed lifted from his shoulders and detached from his neck and yet it was the source of a great pain that held his entire body in an iron grasp.

The bullet had cut a groove in his scalp and his head still bled profusely. His blood was everywhere, soaking his head and neck and shoulders and still leaking from his body, leeching into the ground.

My blood is on the other side of my skin, he dumbly thought.

He was dizzy and had no control over his stomach. In frightening moments his gut heaved and threatened to overtake his life with its launching. Then it did. The heaving motion would not relent and his body shook with paroxysms involuntary. The bouts came without regularity but were still chained with one inciting the next. When his stomach had emptied, the violent attacks continued until finally his stomach was played out and his muscles too exhausted. In the meantime he'd torn away his linen shirt and knotted it around his wounded head as best he could.

"It's the best I can do," he gasped, appealing to no one but desperately pleading none the less.

A sickness passed through him and then dizziness. Jittery, he lay back in case he should fall. He wanted to curl up in innocence, but knew he never would again. He settled into the cool ground and the world stopped turning and he waited to slip from consciousness once again.

It was in daylight when he finally stood and climbed the porch and crossed the threshold through the broken door. Geese followed him, scrutinizing his every movement, as if he were the oddity entering their house and for reasons they neither trusted nor understood.

Inside, the house was in a shambles, the work of the little man. Fragments of utensils, boots, torn paper, and candle molds were strewn about as if disgorged from the open doors of the cabinets and hanging drawers by a furious wind that had been bottled up inside them until they exploded. A stove stood in the middle of the two rooms so to heat both the big kitchen and the front parlor. On the wall was a tear-off calendar.

In the parlor there was a fireplace with a heavy oak mantel. Inside the redbrick fire chamber were the burned remains of a spitted goose. The carpet fluttered with down and was stained with geese droppings, and scattered about were shards of broken dishes and blue crockery. Each step he took raised a white floating in the air, enough down to make a bed mattress. The geese looked at what he looked at and poked their heads in the direction of his face and looked him in the eye as if an explanation would be forthcoming.

As he climbed the stairs he let his fingers drift over the embossed wallpaper. At the upstairs landing his vision blurred and a wave of pain sawed through his head and sat him down to rest. He looked below to see the geese gathering at the foot of the stairs. He closed his eyes and opened them and they cleared for the time. He pulled himself erect and continued on to the hallway.

In the bedroom, at the head of the stairs, was a corded bedstead with turned bulbous posts and a deep featherbed resting atop a thick straw tick. An overstuffed wardrobe stood in one corner. Its doors hung on broken hinges and its dresses, similar in pattern to the little man's disguise, bloomed in the door's opening. The bureau drawers had been dragged from their slots and their contents strewn on the floor. There were so many things in the room. There were more shoes and clothes than he imagined a whole family could own all by itself.

A woman's straw hat was lying on the bed, and a lace handkerchief and a scattered collection of briar and cob pipes and a wild-turkey-wing fan. On the other side of the bed he found the woman who owned the dresses. She sat on the floor propped with her back against the wall. She'd been stabbed in the neck, the bone-handled knife left in the wound, and her swollen intestines filled her lap and spilled over her splayed legs. Her scalp had been cut and ripped away from her head. He felt no shock at what he saw. He felt no horror for what had happened. He was reminded of his own wound and tore a supply of clean garment material to wrap his head in the days to come.

In another room he found a variety of mechanical toys. There were painted cast-metal rabbits that beat tin drums, birds with keys beneath their wings, and when the key was turned and let go their wings beat and they sang tinny songs. There was a monkey who clacked brass cymbals, toy soldiers in flared red coats and blue pantaloons who played cornets, tiny clocks that chimed, and music boxes that'd fit in the palm of your hand. There were two tiny unmade beds against the wall that still held the shape of the small bodies that used to sleep in them.

Outside the air was pure when he staggered into it and he could not breathe enough of it into his lungs. In the barn he found a little mud-tailed pony that was fat and unworked. He found a pail of axle grease and slathered a handful into the wrapping that held his wound. He studied the charred remains of the well house and thought to pull an armful of flowers and drop them inside its column. He knew to do this without ever having done it before. He thought to go back into the house and maybe let toys to fall into its stony black maw. He wondered why he would be moved in this way af-ter all that he'd seen. What was it inside him that would ask him to pause and consider these gestures on behalf of this dead family? He did not know this woman or her children. He did not know whose people they were or if they had been good people or bad people. Surely the children had been good people and the woman had been a good woman, but what were they to him? If the lead ball had been better aimed, he'd be like them. He'd be dead too.

He took time to eat that morning. He killed a goose and pawed open its chest skin. Then he cut away a breast and this he spit-roasted in the fireplace while the other geese watched. He found mustard pickles and a crock of salt pork. He found caps and bullets of the necessary caliber, but he had no gun.

As he ate, he did not wonder on all that had happened thus far, but rather, he wondered how he should think about it. He knew what was in the well and he knew how close he'd come to being there himself. He'd been very stupid and it was a condition he now pledged to avoid. He remembered old Morphew telling him he was in for an education and how he hoped he'd live long enough to tell about it.

He decided he would live without actually deciding it. He just knew he would. Something inside him told him so. He could feel a distance inside his head. He was in pain and his mother always said that pain was weakness leaving the body. He would eat his meal and then he would continue to search for the army and if he should find the little man and the coal black horse he knew what he would do, but once he had, he'd not apologize to the horse. This he swore. He'd not apologize to the horse no matter how right the horse had been in mistrusting the little man.

When he was done eating, he caught onto the mane of

the mud-tailed pony, the children's horse, threw a leg over its back and swung upright. The pony shied and almost sat down for how spoiled it was, but his hands and legs and the words he spoke told the pony it did not belong to itself anymore. It belonged to him. He sat the pony, letting it build its strength beneath his weight. He wanted with all his heart to be past this moment and into the next when he would be healed and would be wiser than he was before. He was learning his lessons and he was still alive and he thought that was worth something.

"Walk," he said to the pony. "Walk on."

However unworked and lazy the pony was, the instant he dug his heels, the pony understood it was to obey and stepped off and then broke into a jarring trot.

In a sack he carried a jar of molasses, dried peaches, a haunch of venison, and handfuls of black walnuts. He had coffee beans and cornmeal. Behind each of his legs hung a goose by its neck. He started north, following the hoof prints of the coal black horse.

5

OT AND DRY, the locusts were sawing the air and the roads were powdery and thick to breathe. He traveled all that day and then slept and woke at sunrise and traveled on again through a thinly settled country. So miserable was the sight of him, his head wrapped in a blood-crusted rag, he determined there was no need he should avoid people.

There were towns he passed through where people came out to watch his passing as if he were an army unto himself and there were other towns where his passing went wholly unnoticed for sakes of commerce or play or worship or conversation. Children older than he stood at the roadside and stared at his passing, and gaunt and pellicle dogs silently trailed him in the dust, lunging the sweltering air. The mud-tailed pony proved to be a sly and insolent animal by nature and sulked and like a spoiled brat exhibited displays of bad temper. It kicked at him when he gave it a chance and attempted to savage his knee with its teeth as he rode, but he remained patient and determined to persuade from it with his heels whatever miles he possibly could.

His head throbbed with pain in the dry heat. The pain wavered through him, consuming his head and neck and shoulders, but he knew he was slowly healing. It was only common sense to him the way the pain made flash upon flash in his body and then peaked and lingered and in some days' time it began to dull and diminish. He discovered hidden beneath his experience of pain an unconfused state where his mind fixed on his mother's counsel and his father's existence and he found new clarity. He admonished himself for breaking every word of advice she'd given him. Except to have followed her imperatives to the letter would have left him afoot not a mile from old Morphew's mercantile. He determined that he would learn from the lessons taught him thus far and by gift of chance he was still alive and from now on he would be a fast and dedicated learner.

The land was beginning to crop with limestone and a darkening green and increasingly there were wells of cold water and burbling springs where he could drink and rinse his body. In the next days he stopped often to wash the wound, fix a new compress, and tie a clean bandage. His chest and back ached as they carried his head pain and each time he removed the wrappings he winced at how strange the sensation as he tore away scab and dried blood from his mending scalp.

The easterly roads turned swampy for some miles while to the northwest lay a range of blue mountains and these he kept to his left and fading behind him as he traveled in the direction of the the rising sun, the direction of the ocean. He rode on, and after the mud-tailed pony played out he left it tied in darkness, entered a banked barn, and stole his first horse, a copper-bottomed mare he quietly led away. After that it became easy enough to do and he felt the need to change mounts at every opportunity, and so by necessity he became an accomplished horse thief, exchanging the copper-bottomed mare for a big cream horse and then for a broad-shouldered, parrot-mouthed chestnut, and then for a sturdy bay with failing eyesight when the chestnut spavined.

Each day his wound dried and knit shut and knotted with building scar that tugged at his scalp, and overly sensitive to light his eyelid would slowly close on him if he let it.

Wounded and face-hideous riding the backs of common horses, he was afforded an easy passage through the places where people lived, a world of boys, old men, and women. They offered him food and water and so miserable he must have looked that if they recognized the horse he rode, they said nothing, so he took their food and asked after the armies and while news was inconsistent, the coal black horse was remembered more than once for its beauty and for the unlikely little woman with the cob pipe that rode its back.

It was in these wounded days the beginning of the man he would grow to be. He bore his pain and endured his wound as if a sign he too had been blooded by the madness that'd taken ahold of the land. He no longer shied from people, from the lone riders, from the reenslaved herded South. He no longer feared their presence on the roads and his conversion was believable to him. He had lived and did not die. He was breathing. Still, it was only the beginning and he was not old enough to know these changes, did not even know enough to think this way yet.

The land had taken on a haunted feel since meeting the goose lady. What had been new and beautiful was now old and strange, wrong and unfamiliar. In one town he sat on a low stone wall and watched boys his own age wearing fresh white linen shirts with hard, starched collars take copperhead snakes from a picnic basket and nail them by their tails to a barn wall. The barn wall had been painted with a black skull over a set of crossed bones. When the boy with the hammer and nails, a boy a head taller than the rest, gave the command each boy let go the copperhead he held by the neck, and yelling and hooting they all ran away.

The snakes swarmed across the face of the door, twining and dangling themselves about each other, dropping their bodies and lifting again. They opened their mouths and bared their fangs. They bit each other thinking to find the source of their pain. The boys laughed and slapped their thighs. Then they began to stone the snakes from safe distance.

An old man with tufts of gray hair springing from his skull, investigating the thumping noise, came to the corner of the barn. In one hand he carried a galvanized bucket and in the other a gutta-percha walking stick. He shook at the boys with his walking stick, castigating them for their grotesque play. They laughed at him and turned their stones on his person. The old man ducked his old head and stumbled in his escape, slopping his trouser leg with spilt whitewash that lipped from the rim of the bucket.

He righted himself and hobbled away, coming in Robey's direction where he sat beside him on the rumbled stone wall. Without introduction and as some people are wont to do, especially the old and foolish, he took up with a left-off and ongoing conversation. He told Robey his old wife had recently died and he was now sad in his heart and considered a lunatic by many in town and had nerve storms because he was alone and because he and his wife, he said, wanted to die together.

"Her eyes were always the brightest," he said.

The old man still possessed his teeth, remarkable for one so elderly, but they seemed to protrude straight from his gums and closed in a beak that his thin lips rode. He paused to sneeze and when he opened the palm of his hand mucus webbed his fingers.

"Those boys are quite exceptional in their stupidity," he remarked, but Robey continued to make no response: no word, no nod, no shrug of his shoulders. Where they sat the stone was warm with captured sun and not uncomfortable. He did not mind the old man, and after a time in his presence the old man seemed calm and less agitated.

"Their time is coming soon enough," the old man added, his words swashing in his beaked mouth, but still Robey made no response. He thought, Let the old man talk himself out.

But the old man persevered in his one-sided conversation, prattling on and occasionally pausing to ask Robey if he was listening. He took Robey for a young soldier and so talked about having fought in Spain with Napoleon when he was in his youth. He claimed to have eaten dead horses to stay alive and one time to have actually eaten the forearm of a dead man. He told how he found it very sweet and for that reason had to swear it off because he feared he would get a taste for human flesh.

"More was not enough," he said, and then he speculated on the hell he would surely go to after his death for eating human beings, as well as for other unnamed transgressions, and at this thought he laughed.

From the barn door continued the hollow resounding of the thrown stones. From the inside came squeals of pigs and the fierce rustling of their bodies. One by one the snakes dropped their heads and their broken angular bodies hung limp. The boys carried on with pitching their stones, breaking the snakes' bodies, until the cut bloodless pieces fell away and gathered on a bed of chaffy earth.

"Are you listening to me?" the old man demanded.

Robey took a deep breath to say he was.

"You have also done bad things," the old man said. "Bad men can talk to each other. Bad men can understand the other. For thousands of years we have understood this, but that doesn't change anything."

"No," Robey said, regretful at having spoken even as he spoke. "I haven't," he continued, and he knew the sound of his voice betrayed his words.

"Maybe not yet," the old man said. "But you will. You are experiencing one of life's great lessons. Specifically which one, you do not know, but in time you will know."

IN ANOTHER TOWN was a baseball game and he had never seen such before so he stopped to watch. When he became noticed he moved on again, content with only the witless beeves and skulking dogs and mild cows watching his slow passage.

He continued to think about what else the old man had said to him. The old man told how he was now worthless and no good to anyone anymore because he was filled with despair, and despair was useless in times such as these. He told him to remain angry, because anger was more useful than despair and would deliver him. But to despair would surely lead to failure and tragedy.

They were the words of an insane, but he could not escape

them. They were committed to his mind and once learned he could not unlearn them. It was fate, he thought. Then he thought how people loved to talk so very much and even had a weakness to talk. He himself had done so and it made him laugh at how foolish his gliding mind. The bay shortened and tossed its head at his sudden outburst. He quieted the animal and let his hand to the long-barreled pistol he wore in his belt. It was an odd piece of indeterminate make and had been a gift from the maundering old man.

He traveled on, following the rumors of great armies encamped to the east on opposite banks of a river, but in the days that came his long slow ride through the landscape of war became so like chasing the wind that when one night a cold wind swept the open land, he took refuge in the scorched shell of a burned house.

The bay tethered, he entered cautiously, as if testing the floorboards. Outside its stone walls was a constant moaning of the soft wind streaming through the trees. He had at first mistaken the pump in the yard to be the black silhouette of a figure, and even after he knew his mistake he kept looking to the yard to assure himself it was not, kept looking to the trees where the bay was tethered.

He lit a tallow candle inside a box lantern of punched tin and cautiously passed from one room to another and upon determining that he was alone in the house, he built a tiny fire in the hearth and it soon lit the room with a warm glow. He reclined on the hardwood floor and with the fire's coax the aches of the day began to melt from his limbs. There was a burned stairway to the second floor and from the fire-gutted ceiling hung a beautiful chandelier, its pendants like carved diamonds.

At first he had thought it a spangle of stars in the night sky and then he understood it was the stars through the room's charred ceiling and the shaped and fitted glass that gave to him such a sparkling sight. He could only think that someone had hung the glass after the burning for how its icicles were clear and untouched and cast prisms of light from the fire.

The wind outside died away and ceased its quiet moaning in the trees. The sound had existed beneath sound and he'd forgotten it until now it was disappeared. In the new silence came a ticktock sound, ticktock. He searched the room to find its source and then was a clean and unlikely striking sound and a tiny door unlatched and he found the source just as the cuckoo shot forth.

Someone had wound the clock and hung the chandelier, and however pitiful the gestures, they were trying to return to a time that he was afraid they would never see again. It was a time on earth he realized that he himself had never witnessed because of his seclusion on the mountain, but was seeing it now in its havoc and devastation. What was life like before all this? What did people do and what did they think about before they warred and thought about war? He tried to remember what he did before he left the mountain and what he thought about in his seclusion. He recalled chores and quiet and solitude. He knew there was more than that, but he could not remember and he knew it had not been so far back in time. He tried hard to recall who he had been and what he was back then then, but however much he longed to he could find nothing to remember.

He banked his small fire with the kindling he'd gathered, the wood spurting blue and red flame, and the room took on more light and he found other moments of longing and desire. There was a wooden inlaid box filled with shiny stones. There were other boxes, tin and copper and lacquered, and woods he did not recognize and could not name. Inside their shells were coins and buttons, ribbons, marbles, pins, tiny bones, a doll's leg.

There was a mildewed bench with a hinged seat and while the inside was empty, its interior smelled of wool and lavender and contained a porcelain-faced doll wearing a blue felt hat and long hair made of straw-colored yarn. A leg had been torn away from the torso, but when he polished the dirty face with his sleeve it shown in the firelight as if newly made. In the silence, the burning wood made hissing and cracking noises and there was a sudden flicker of shadow in the air as vesper bats took flight and filled the chamber with their silent wing beats, black on black, spearing the air and fleeing the lighted room through the empty doors and windows.

He set a pot of coffee to boil and fried the last of his bacon in a tin pan. He made a thin dough of water and salted cornmeal and set that to bake in the open fire on the blade of a broken hoe. He thought how he'd boil his coffee and scumble his biscuit into it. That would taste fine and feel good in his mouth and warm his throat down into his belly. His hunger grew and as the food heated he fixed his gaze on the porcelain-faced doll he'd propped at the fireside. Absentmindedly, he rubbed his scalp where the healing skin felt as if pulled by tiny paws. He fit the doll's leg to her hip and it matched.

He wanted to feel the hatred that possessed him when he dragged himself off the ground that was drenched with his blood. He wanted the anger the old man told him he must have to survive. He wanted it lodged inside him like an iron spike, but tonight it wasn't there. Tonight he was too tired to hate and hoped in the morning when he was rested he would hate again.

"What do you have to say?" he asked the porcelain-faced doll, and when there was no reply he whispered the word "nothing."

When the coffee was boiled he poured half a cup into the drippings and could not wait, but was so hungry he burned his fingers and mouth. He slid the cake off the hoe into the gravy and ate the slurry with his fingers. He scraped the sides and the rapidly cooling bottom of the pan with the backs of his fingers and licked them clean and wiped at his mouth and then licked the back of his hand and then it was over. He knew enough to know he'd eaten like a ravenous dog and how disapproving his mother would be if she had witnessed such and how nice it would be to someday again not eat like that.

"Soon," he sighed, and sat close by the fire, exhausted for how voracious his hunger had made him and still amazed at how quickly the food had disappeared. He knew he should climb the stairs to sleep, or crawl under the floor, or go outside and sleep with the horse. He could not help but mistrust the dead calm stillness of this night's windless turn.

But his belly was full and he was tired and wanted to sleep and for so long now he had been vigilant. He closed his eyes and bars of fire darted across his eyelids. Sleep came and overwhelmed him as if a slowly crushing weight, though he fought it the best he could. Its strong hand brought ache and defeat and then relief, and when he knew he could not hold it off any longer he finally collapsed beneath it.

When he lurched forward he saw the fire in the hearth had died and gone to the an orange glow of mere embers. The porcelain-faced doll was slumped beside the fire as if she too had been asleep. He righted her and as he stood to stretch his aching body, he concentrated on the faint sound that had awakened him. A muscle in his stomach began to flutter. Then he heard the sound coming from outside the stone walls. It was a man goading an ox, and then came the scrape of a travois on the hard ground and then a woman's voice, thin and plaintive, complaining how difficult her situation. He kicked at the fire and stamped out the sparks. He gathered his kit as quickly as he could and as they were almost in the yard, he could do no other than climb the charred stringers and escape to the second floor.

6

A T THE TOP of the stairwell, the roof was open to the sky and the weakened and ravaged second floor was cast in the shadows of the stone-built gable walls. Up there the night was not so dark under the sky, and from where he stood in the gable shadows he could see an ambling gaunted ox approaching the house. There was a man and a girl attendant. They were walking beside the ox, and riding on the jouncing travois was a woman. She was large and rode as if in repose, but when the ox stopped she slowly climbed erect and clasping her hands under her belly she lifted its weight as if she were lifting herself. The girl hastened to help the woman stand and the woman thanked her. The man told them this was the place from where he smelled the fire and the bacon and the coffee cooking. He made a show of sniffing the air and then a scraping cough from depths of his chest expanse doubled him over. The man was otherwise robust and wore a born thickness in his wrists and neck and shoulders. He was built wide and drumlike and conducted himself with raptorlike self-regard.

"You get a fire started," he said to the girl, pushing her in the direction of the doorway. The girl stumbled and cursed him over her shoulder as she went inside and then the man led the woman inside, and through the fire-ravaged second floor he could watch the progress of their spectral shapes passing underneath him, moving from place to place as if they were blown by a steady wind.

The girl found embers in the fire he'd left and momentarily looked about but made no mention of them to the man and woman. She stirred the embers to red life with an iron rod. She fed the fire with one of the small wooden boxes and in the first light that held her he could not see her face because it was flanked by her hair, but when she drew her hair together and draped it to one side he could see how thin and hollow her young face.

"I fear we've reached bedrock," the woman moaned. She held her arms stretched out before her as if discovering her next place in the air while she moved in the direction of the fire's warmth. Her hands found her way and she eased herself onto her knees on the bare wooden floor, touched the floor with her hands, and settled on her hip.

"Get the parfleches," the man said to the girl.

He spoke to her harshly and she responded in kind, as if an old enmity festered between them. The man fished in a gunny-sack until he found a green bottle, which he held between himself and the firelight to measure its content. He then uncorked the bottle and took a drink. In the light of the fire he could be seen for his sparse white hair, his powerful neck, his white muttonchops and all black livery. Some minor affliction was tormenting his leg as he kept scratching and cuffing at it. After a second drink he gave a final cough and seemed content.

"Get them yourself," the girl said, not moving from the fire she was kindling to life.

"If I have to get them you're going to get it good," he told her.

"They empty," the girl said, and the woman groaned, clutching at her swollen sides.

"Don't sass me," the man said, crossing the room to strike the girl a fierce blow that knocked her down when she stood to meet him. Robey flinched, watching.

"It's her time," the girl said, as she cowered on the floor.

"It ain't her time," the man said, taking another drink. "It ain't her time until I say it's her time."

Robey's body pressed more tightly to the stone wall of the standing gable as he watched them move underneath him. He let his hand to the grips of the pistol he carried in his belt, its long barrel extending past his hip. The wood of the grips was smooth and the chambers were recently primed. He would not be shot again. That knowledge was as deep in his bones as a knowing could possibly be.

"There'll be a black frost tonight," the man said, and then surveying the empty room, he said, "I wonder where they went off to? They couldn't have gone off for very long."

"They probably scared off when they heard us coming," the girl said, her voice a bitter sulk. "There won't be any frost," she said, as if it was the most recent of crazy ideas.

"Help me with these boots," the man said, sitting on the bench. "Or I'll lick you again."

The girl stood and approached him warily and then she was tugging at his boots and letting each of them drop to the floor. The man then paced the room in his stockinged feet, scratching at his leg again. He told the girl to get busy and gather up what would burn so at least they should not freeze to death on this cold spring night.

"It ain't gonna freeze," she said as she found another of the boxes. This one she studied for a moment without opening it and then set it gently in the fire. She then found the cuckoo clock and this too she placed in the rising flames.

"That there too," the man said, indicating the bench with the hinged seat. "That's wood. That'll burn good."

The girl tipped the bench over and began kicking at it until its wooden pegs broke loose and it came apart at the joints. While she worked, the man stood in the center of the room drinking from the green bottle and to his own amusement began whistling poor imitations of night birds, the more complicated ones requiring him to pocket the bottle so to twine his fingers and cock his clasped hands. He waited, but he received no countercalls.

Then, bored with that, he picked up a piece of lath and swatted at the chandelier, making a game of breaking its tiniest glass pendants. Then he stopped at the girl who knelt at the hearth feeding the broken bench into the fire. She stiffened as he lifted a lock of hair from her neck and whispered something into her ear.

"You're just a dirty dog," she said, and swung around and hit him on the head with the iron rod she held. Stung so, he screamed and ran out of the house holding his head.

"What happened," the woman cried out, sweeping the air with her arms as if pushing the invisible. "What's going on in here?"

"It were just a dirty scoundrel dog," the girl said with disgust. "Don't be so nerve-raw all the time."

"A dog?" the woman cried. "What dog? How did a dog get in here? I don't like dogs one bit."

From behind the stone of the gable wall, Robey could see the man in the yard where he skulked about in the darkness for a time. He wandered in the direction of the bay but stopped well short of its hiding place. He tried the pump and when the handle broke off in his hand he kicked at it and staggered.

Below where he stood, the girl worked to make the blind woman comfortable near the warmth of the fire. The woman kept asking what of the dog, but the girl hushed her and would say no more about it.

When the man returned, it was as if nothing had happened between him and the girl. He sat on the floor in the same place where Robey had fallen asleep and by primitive gesture appeared to sense there had been another presence resting in that same spot against the wall. But then he settled as the odd moment passed. From his pocket he produced a handful of hardtack and breaking off piece after piece he fed them silently into his mouth. The dry crumbs that flecked his black coat he plucked from the material and fastidiously licked from his fingertips.

"If I had my choice," he pronounced, "I would have goose and oysters and scrambled eggs and pecan pie."

"If," the girl scoffed. "If frogs had wings they wouldn't bump their asses every time they jumped."

The man cackled and slapped at his leg. Then he skimmed a piece of hardtack across the floor in the direction of the fire where the girl scrambled for it and held it to her chest.

"What's that?" the woman said, near hysterical, fanning the air close to the floor with her hands.

"Nothing," the girl said, sucking on the piece of hardtack so not to make noise.

"Don't you tell me nothing," the woman said. "I am not stupid. I know there's rats in here."

"We can spit-cook that chicken you got hid up," the girl said to the man.

"What chicken?"

"The chicken what you got hid up."

"But it is my chicken," the man said, philosophically.

"I was the one that stol'd it," the girl said.

"I am so hungry," the woman groaned. "Please cook the chicken."

"At least feed your woman," the girl said.

"Please," the woman said again, and the man scratched his head as if it were a proposition that required deep thought. Eventually he must have decided because he opened his coat and took from inside the carcass of a chicken he wore strung on a rope around his neck.

"Take the god damn chicken," he said, throwing it to the girl.

Robey watched as the girl plucked and gutted the chicken, setting its innards aside on the hearthstone. She then skewered the carcass with the iron rod and held it over the flames. As its skin heated and blistered, fats dropped into the flames where they hissed and flared. The man drew near to her and together they watched it cook.

When the woman asked, the man took it upon himself to explain to her what was happening. She informed him that although she was blind, she could still hear and she could still smell. The man looked at her as if it was news to him while the girl snickered behind her hand.

"What I'm asking is it done yet?"

"Soon," the man said.

After they ate the chicken, the room became a pleasant scene as their need for anger and violence toward each other appeared to have been satisfied with food. The woman said something to the girl he could not hear but watched as the girl assisted the woman to her feet and guided her through the rubble into the yard where the woman gathered her skirts in her hands and squatted down to make water. Then the girl gathered her own skirts to her waist and did the same.

When they returned, the man helped the girl make beds on the edge of the warmed hearth stones, close to the flames. The girl eased the woman to her side and covered her with a woolen blanket and then she let herself down not far away from the woman and pulled her own blanket to her chin. It was then she discovered the porcelain-faced doll and in an instant pulled it to her chest and had it hidden beneath her blanket cover.

Once settled the man insisted they pray before sleep. His words were those of the sincere and well-practiced divine. Robey listened to the man's holy and dramatic pronouncements. A strange man of the cloth. If only, when he ceased his praying, they would fall asleep, because Robey was tired and his legs ached for standing so still for so long. If they slept he could slip down the stringer and be gone in the darkness.

But the man upon finishing his prayer took up his green bottle again and continued with his drinking. Still agitated by his leg, he shook it beneath his blanket, banging the floor with his heel. Then he stood and set to a fretful pacing again until finally some thought occurred to him and he took down his trousers to inspect the spot he'd been itching.

"God damn tick," he slurred.

He shuffled to the fireside where he took the iron rod from the fire and held its red-hot point to his naked leg. The smell of burning hair and flesh rose to where Robey stood against the gable wall and in the closed light he could see the man, a grimace stretched tightly across his mouth and his eyes no more than black holes in his face as he held the red iron to his thigh, causing the tick to back out of his hide.

Through the floor he watched the man who remained naked from the waist down. The man lolled his head back and forth like an angry bull slicing the air with his horns. He then tipped the bottle back and emptied it. He pulled up his trousers and resumed his pacing, from time to time raising his burned leg and shaking it. His leg now relieved, he seemed conflicted with some new thinking that was growing inside him. He lay down on his bedding, but he was too restless for sleep.

Robey waited patiently, hoping the man would settle as had the girl and the woman, and soon he would be able to slip down the stringer and away in the darkness. He looked to the rickety sawtooth he would have to descend and then looked off the gable wall in the direction of his anticipated departure and then back down through the floor. The man was up again. He was moving about the room. This time, he was on all fours and slowly scuttling toward the sleeping girl, tucking his legs underneath him, reaching forward and pulling his body to his reach. Turning in her sleep, the girl awoke as he made his approach. She watched him coming to her, a hand to her mouth.

"Are you a-sleepin'?" he was saying as he crawled toward her. "Are you already a-sleepin'?"

But she did not answer and when he was near enough she pulled back the blanket and kicked out at him. He caught her small foot as it struck into his head. He held that foot and when she kicked with the other one he caught that foot too and dragged her from her bedding and into him so quickly she seemed to have disappeared inside him.

At first she did not know to resist, but then she fought him, her body coiling and twisting on the wooden floor. She struck out with her fists and tore at his white face-hair and he fended her off, trying to quiet her, but she would not relent so he wrapped an arm around her neck and punched her in the face.

Still, she kept struggling and so he punched her again until she groaned and folded in his arms. He punched her one more time and then let her onto her back where she did not move. He waited and then he lifted her skirts and tore away at her underclothes until she too was naked from the waist. But when he moved between her legs she roused herself and fought him again. She kicked her heels into his haunches, arched her back, and clawed at his face. He took her thin arms in his hands and twisted them until she cried out and then he stretched them over her head and held her arms as she continued to kick, but he was now between her legs and so wide was his body she could not find the angle to strike with her heels.

"You help me here. Now," he yelled out to the blind woman. "She has gone crazy in the head."

At first the woman cried and fretted and when he threatened her she dug more deeply into her bedding.

"Take her damn legs," he said, but the woman would not move.

"You're hurting me," the girl moaned.

"I don't give a god damn if I am," he said, and struck her a blow to the side of her head.

Her cries of pain and her pleading with the man to leave off her rose up from the cold floor and filled the stone-walled chamber. The man pushed himself up on one hand and with the other he struck the girl a savage blow to the head and she went quiet again. He gripped her by the hair and pulled back her head revealing her white throat.

Then the moon went behind the clouds and all was lost in shadow, and the wind came up and there were the faintest sounds of the man working and the girl whimpering beneath him like a small held animal. Robey let his head back against the stone of the gable, his hand on the butt of his pistol. The sounds from below broke inside him and then hardened and the hard pieces—they broke too. He banged his head again and this second time cracked open his wound. He began to bleed into his collar. He knew he should do something and he knew he would not.

When the man was done he slumped and lay quietly across the girl's trembling body and then he fell back from between her legs as if tearing himself from her. Panting for air, he crawled across the floor to lay on his pallet where he went into a fit of sneezing and cursing and then was silent. He reached down between his legs to cradle himself in his hand and soon harsh sounds of sleep came from his throat.

The girl lay crumpled in the moonlight, her bare legs white as bone. Then she curled her legs inside her skirts and folded her knees to her chest and held them in her arms.

Robey waited until he thought they were all deep in the sounds of their sleep and then catlike he went down the stringer where he paused over the sleeping bodies, scrutinizing one and then the next, the pistol in his hand, its barrel pointing the way.

When he stood by the girl, he found her still awake and she raised to him a thin, worn and childish face. At first she seemed to have lost all touch with the earth. She just lay there staring up at him, staring at nothing, not blinking, or breathing, or speaking, or whispering. She had been so harmed, maybe she had died.

As their eyes fixed on each other, the moon came out again and thinned the darkness near the floor and shone on her face. Her lips were broken and she was bleeding from her nose. She caught her lower lip between her teeth and he thought she did die and was just now returning herself to the living. In her eyes there was condensed hatred that had split off inside her and she could not return from, could not return to, sadness or pain or joy or any other emotion. It was there inside her where it would stay.

She paled and her mouth opened as she stared at him, but her heart so full, her voice failed her, and in that stony world was only heard a moan of the soughing wind.

Ashamed, he draped the blanket over her closed body. He then hastened from her side and passed silently among their bodies and left out of that place to find the bay horse tethered in the coppice of trees. All that night he followed the bends of the black road jeweled by starlight until the wan light of the dawn touched the east with red and the pastures turned green. The roads became white and then was the coming gold of the sun and that day's worth of heat, and he was miles away before he stopped to sleep.

7

T HEN, IN A RAILWAY CUT, the bed of cinders gave way and the bay horse, near to blind, went down, tumbling him to the ground and with its fall was the cracking sound of snapping bone. At the last instant he had pulled the animal's head back and it had tried to check its fall on its stiff forelegs, but it was too late to stop what was already happening.

The horse's hind leg was trapped under the rail where the ballast had eroded, but still it thrashed and pawed to right itself. Its shod hooves struck sparks on the parallel rail and thudded on the ties. The bay's right front leg was as if jointed between the knee and fetlock, and it swung wildly as it heaved its body, trying to stand until finally the splintered cannon bone stabbed through the leg hide, white and ragged and sharp as a pickax.

He stood a ways off and spoke to the horse, telling it to settle, and when it did not he moved in to take the horse's tossing head in his arms and cover its terrified eyes. He held on as the strength in its neck dragged his feet and lifted him off the ground. Then it did settle and there was a panting silence between them and he let go his hold. The horse stretched its neck and sniffed him. He stroked the horse's cheek and forehead and did not let go his touch.

"You have gone and broke your leg," he whispered into its ear, his face that close.

The horse lay on its side staring at him. Its skin quivered and it snorted and he took this as a sign of understanding. He knelt down in the cinders and put his face to the horse's soft neck, his hand to the velvety muzzle and he told the horse how not to be afraid and it was only then he felt his own ankle begin to throb inside his shoe and he silently cursed.

The horse raised its head and then let it down again in the cinders where its wet breathing made gusts of dirt and grit. He told the horse it had been a good horse and a loyal horse and a noble horse and when he found the coal black horse he would tell it so, and when he returned home he would tell the other animals and then he felt foolish and tears welled in his eyes. A shank of anger entered his chest and the tears began to sting his eyes.

He stood and formally apologized to the bay horse, asking that it might disremember his boyish thoughts and actions. He asked that it might forgive his momentary weakness, for they'd been on good terms since he'd stole it and then regretfully he collected himself and drew his pistol from his belt. He set the muzzle behind the horse's ear and held not a moment before pulling the trigger.

He wanted to rest after that because he was painfully tired and sore, but spiritless he shouldered his kit and took the bridle and trudged on for the duration of that hot day through a sparsely settled country, his sprained ankle paining him not a little. He was soon road-dirty and his soles blistered.

He followed the train tracks until evening shed a bluish twilight over the land and far off could be seen the white spire of a church steeple and then the dim lights of a town. He climbed a grassy bank in the town's direction and stepped out onto a plank road running parallel with the rails below. The town, now within reach, glowed dully in the glove of the night. He took up the plank road and after not long his shoe broke open and began to flop as he walked. After so long his journey and however bleak his prospects, he knew he was arriving at a place significant. He felt it in the air, in his skin, inside his composing mind. He knew he needed to find another horse.

In the distance was the drift of small hills and green islands of pasture running into abrupt mountains and there was the cool dank smell of a flat river on the air, and even further, a purple line of forest between the mountains and the green islands of pasture. The country here was cultivated with prosperous farms and the low-walled buildings were of red brick or gray stone. The roadside was crossed by veins of limestone forming knotty points and there were thin cracks where artesian springs seeped water to the earth's surface. He thought how easy it would be to farm this deep fertile land. A warm rain had begun to fall on the dry land and then from out of the dark he heard the cadence of hoof beats pounding hard on the planks.

He stepped off the road and onto the soft ground where he stumbled across deep ruts and passed into a thicket of brambles in the twilight shadows of a little paintless house. Two dark riders swept through the gloaming, and then cavalry by twos passed the brake and then was the heavy sound of iron-shod wheels grating on the planks, and a wagon came jolting out of the darkness, winding through the trees, the lathered team flat-out for speed.

It was an open four-horse coach with seats across from door to door and nine men dressed in blue were riding the benches, and behind that wagon was another one and then came ten more after that. Without hesitating he stripped off his jacket and worked to turn it inside out blue. More wagons followed the coaches and cavalry and a battery of horse artillery. He climbed higher from the road, a steep ascent made craggy with broken rock and dark with pine trees.

From there he could smell wisps of smoke and cresting the low rise he could see the town sprawled out beneath him where a river made a great oxbow turn, and at the extreme arc of its curvature, crossing the river twice, were the railroad tracks nicking past beneath the night's first veil. There were engine houses, water towers, and fueling stations. There was the meander of inbound dirt roads feeding plank pikes cut straight as dies. Wagons and soldiers were converging on the town from all directions, their dashing black shapes spectral in the last bands of red light that seamed the western horizon. A cold fog was drifting in and had begun to numb and wet the empty fields.

The pain in his ankle dulled with the night's cooling and it no longer concerned him. He knew he was now near to something big, an army, a battle, a horse. He felt himself on the very edge of the fields of war, the ever-moving place of grinding violence whose turbulent wake he'd been following for days. The winding river, the rails, the hard-riding cavalry told him so, and he had little idea how deep he was or how far they sprawled before him. No matter the distance, no matter the depth, he'd come so far, and no matter what he'd been through he concluded he was at the beginning once again.

He did not know what to do right away, so he sat down and held his arms clasped round his folded legs, his chin on his knees. Where before he'd been desperate to travel and driven foolish in his decisions, he now felt a calming patience hard learned. The rain was falling more heavily and was cold and the air turned unseasonably bitter, and he had the passing notion he was going to freeze to death, but he knew it was fatigue and hunger and the lingering effects of his head wound. He felt the darkness pressing his eyelids and there unconsciousness momentarily caught him.

His short dream was the brief and repeated experience of falling without end. Each time he fell, he could not stop himself no matter how hard he tried. He was shot and falling to the ground. He was tumbling past the windlass and falling into the tomb of the well. He was falling from the coal black horse. He knew he was dreaming even as he dreamt. He murmured and called out to himself but could not break through to consciousness. When he did wake he did not know that he had even slept, but he awoke in darkness and a heavy shoe was kicking at his swollen ankle.

"What are you," came a hollow voice from over his head.

The voice was coming at him from a great distance and he could not see its source. It was as if he'd awakened at the bottom of a pitch-black well. As he found wakefulness he felt himself arriving for a long time until he understood it was a soldier's voice asking the question and the soldier was now prodding him at the leg with the point of his bayonet. When he did not answer the soldier's question, the soldier set the point of a bayonet against his thigh and pressed. He could not feel the pain for how frightened he was at the shock of discovery. The soldier leaned harder and his leg spasmed and kicked when the blade went into his skin.

"I know'd you weren't dead," the soldier said with delight. "What's your purpose and I don't want to hear any lies come out of your mouth."

He looked up and saw standing over him a man dressed in a blue uniform and his heart went cold. The soldier wore a thin black beard and gold-rimmed eye glasses and off his shoulder was the rising moon. The soldier stepped back so he might stand, and when he did the soldier flicked open the shell jacket with the point of the bayonet revealing its dyed interior. The soldier relieved him of the pistol he wore in his belt and his knife and then they waited not long before another soldier walked in on them.

Immediately the two soldiers disagreed over the appropriate password and this issue they debated between themselves for an inordinate amount of time. Each claimed his was the new password and the other was still using the old password. Without arriving at any satisfactory conclusion as to what course of events they should pursue, they finally lost interest and let it drop and turned their attention to Robey.

"You got any money hid?" the second soldier asked. "Got any 'backy? You rebs always got 'backy."

Robey shook his head no, in reply.

"He don't talk?" the second soldier asked of the first.

"He ain't talked yet, 'cept in his sleep."

"What'd he say?"

"I don't talk sleep so's I don't know."

"Cat got your tongue?" the second soldier said to Robey.

Again he shook his head and the second soldier snickered.

"Maybe he's got a head full of cotton," the second soldier said. "By God, he'll talk when they stick a rope around his neck."

"He's just a boy," the first soldier said.

"A boy'll kill you as dead as anyone else," the second soldier said. He then unfolded his pocketknife and slipped the blade into each of Robey's pockets and sliced them open.

"He ain't got nothing," the first soldier said, impatient to be relieved of sentry duty and already tired of the responsibility of the prisoner he'd taken on.

They determined that maybe he was not the curiosity they'd thought he was, but still, the coat was suspicious enough and he was armed and so should be delivered to the major. The second soldier told him to cross his hands behind his back and then tied his arms at the wrist with a piece of twine and twisted the bindings tight with a stub of wood he carried. Then the first soldier indicated with his bayonet that he was to move in the direction of the town below where torches had been lit and the streets were bright and lined with wagons.

The walk down the hill was a torment to his swollen ankle now that it'd been put back to work. He stumbled in the tufted grass and tripped and the soldier accompanying him prodded him at times and at other times assisted him as if he could not decide which way to treat him.

Eventually they reached the town and as they passed through the narrow streets, curtains were folded back and squares of pale yellow light showed from small-paned windows. Soldiers were everywhere in the streets and wagons were positioned to barricade side lanes and alleys. Soldiers stood posted at the junction of intersections. They milled about in conversation and squatted on the ground wrapped in oilcloths, hunkered against the rain.

Stable hands and draymen sat in the clutter of hand trucks and upturned carts, their shafts thrust into the air. They were eating crackers and cheese, scraping out cans of sardines with the backs of their crooked fingers, licking them clean and lighting cigarettes. A large poland hog, its throat already slit and blood gushing to the cobbles, was being clubbed to its side with an axe and slaughtered in the street under a dozen knives. Soldiers roamed in kitchen gardens, stabbing the earth with bayonets looking for silver plate, gold coins, and jewels. Many of the them conversed in languages he had never heard before and all seemed used to the chaos that swirled around them. Tonight this town and a few days ago it was another town and in a few days it'd be a third and they'd do it all over again.

In one garden there were soldiers eerily lit by an oil lamp and tied to a tree branch by their wrists and gagged with bayonets.

"They're drunkards," the soldier told him without being asked.

From an alley came a shriek that stopped them and when they looked into its darkness they could see a cabal of soldiers lifting the skirts of a servant woman to see if her master had hidden any money or jewels close to her body. When they found none they still did not let her skirt down, but began to cut away its folds with their clasp knives.

"You're too young to see that," the soldier said, and prodded him in the back that he should continue along.

More cavalry were arriving by the minute, unsaddling their

lathered mounts and tethering them to bayonets stabbed in the ground. The soldier stopped him, handed him his rifle, and held to his shoulder as he bent to pick some gravel out of his shoe. Where they paused, a shutter flapped open and a woman's head filled the opening, her hair let down and draping her shoulders. Soldiers milled at the wooden steps to the side entrance of her house. A sentry, sitting by its closed door, occupied himself by tossing his hat in the air and catching it. One soldier laughed and observed to another that he didn't think the town would have any old maids left after tonight.

Peddlers moved amongst the soldiers and queued at the women's doorways, hawking their common wares of writing paper, sewing kits, candy, and tobacco. Knots of teamsters paced about, smoking and restless with their prolonged wait while the draft horses stood shifting in harness. Ahead of them lanterns hissed as their reflectors threw coves of light that cut into the cold and drizzle and showed stockpiles of lumber, kegs of nails, horseshoes. Sacks of oats, potatoes, and flour were already loaded in the wagons. There were ducks, chickens, and turkeys in slatted crates. Beef calves blatted for their feed of milk.

The light they passed through showed a gang of black men dressed in rags and cast-offs standing quietly on a long expanse of railroad platform. The men of the perimeter were made to hold up a rope that encircled the lot of them and outside the rope there were soldiers with sharp-edged bayonets fixed to form a hedge of steel blades pointed at their chests.

A soldier with a megaphone was warning them that if a single nigger hand should ever let go the rope and it should fall below their waists, they'd all be shot where they stood.

They continued to wind through the back streets, seemingly lost in their maze, when finally they came to a large square, the majority of which was taken up by a dry stone fountain and at the head of the square, behind a tall wrought-iron fence, was their destination. An immense house glared with white lights that emanated from three tall windows across each story. Rising to the house's deep-set front door was a half-story granite stoop manned by guards and under which was an entrance below ground for tradesmen and servants.

They climbed the stairs and entered into a foyer where the light softened and filtered through an interior door's glass panel. A guard opened the interior door and told them to wait where they were and shut the door on them. Then the guard came back, opened the door, and led them into a hallway, where an old woman greeted them. She wore a white veil and white gloves. Around her neck was a string of pearls and each pearl was the size of a marble. Behind her stood a maid and coming up behind the maid was a young officer. He carried before him a wide leather book stuffed with papers.

The old woman told them they'd have to wait as the major had yet to arrive but was anticipated shortly. She told them there were others seeking an audience with the major and she was looking forward to meeting him herself, as if the occasion was not military occupation but one of a social nature. His guard and the young officer with the book of papers exchanged irritated looks and exasperated, the young officer swirled a finger next to his head.

"Go ahead," the young officer said, resigned to the old woman's hospitality. "It's her house. We are here as her guests."

Her intentions affirmed, the old woman glowed. Gracefully she showed them down the hall and through a doorway where inside the parlor, the blended fumes of tobacco and whiskey and the heat of the room's wood fire overwhelmed him. There were other people in the room, standing and sitting, and these he avoided with his eyes. He asked his guard that he might sit and the guard agreed to let him.

Here they waited in the company of more guards, bored and hardened men standing at ease and, oddly enough, talking about shooting quail. Inside, the house was as if outfitted from the China trade. There were silver clocks and rosewood tables, enameled screens and porcelain vases blooming with peacock feathers. He imagined each room like this one: crystal chandeliers, dark paintings hung in ornate frames, the embossed spines of books, silver snuff boxes, upholstered furniture, and heavy curtains misty with condensation.

His brain began to unreel. The heated room was slipping from his mind. Could this be what people were fighting over, the many possessions that surrounded him? These objects with so much value and so little use? He thought how the sweep of a hand or the lick of a flame and they would be broken and burned. Maybe it was the weak and the fragile and the beautiful that made you the craziest and made you fight the hardest.

From the hallway came the commotion of opening doors and crossing the parlor's threshold, the words of an angry exchange. Robey was tired and hungry, but he was not concerned. He knew he would be delivered. He did not know why he knew it, but he knew this was not the end of his journey.

"What kind of dodge is this?" a voice came from the hallway. It was the young officer with the leather book of papers.

"He says he wants to hold a prayer meeting," the old woman was saying, "and is here to seek the major for his permission."

"He's the worst in love with God of any man I ever known," said a woman's urgent voice. "He prays on his knees and sometimes his eyeballs roll around backward inside his head."

"I'd like to see that," the old woman said solemnly.

"But, ma'am," the young officer said with all possible forbearance, "we don't want a prayer meeting."

"Well, why not?" the old woman declared. "I can think of nothing more appropriate."

"He has a mighty voice," the woman said. "Sometimes when he prays it's so awful powerful he has to put his face in a cracker box."

"Put them in the parlor," the young officer said in exasperation, and then commanded that the guard in the parlor be increased.

When Robey saw the girl, she was following behind the man in all-black livery with white hair and white mutton-chops bushing his cheeks, and behind them was the blind woman, haggard and tired. The man was pink-faced and wore shoulders that rounded above his chest. He limped in one leg, but it did not seem the limp of a real injury. Robey could feel himself in the direction of the man's wicked little eyes as they scanned the room. The girl had lightened her skin with the slightest stroke of chalk powder and reddened her hard shallow cheeks but could do little about her broken lips.

The soldier guarding him leaned down and whispered how her appearance surely did not go against her. Another of the guards caught the eye of the girl, hooked a finger inside his cheek, and made a popping noise. He then smiled and kissed his fingertips. Her panicked eyes flew to Robey's where they stayed, and then they dulled and grayed.

8

HEN THE MAJOR ARRIVED he was carrying his watch in hand and Robey was made to stand as the major, shedding his oilcloth, entered the parlor. The major's head was large and his face was shaped flat and pale. His eyebrows were great white wings that flared dramatically from his brow as if threatening flight from the surface of his forehead. He was by appearance a horseman, for he was bow-legged and walked with his legs turned outward and his toes turned in. He handed his sword to one of the guards, took off his cap, and said to the old woman shadowing him that, yes, a broiled chicken would delight him to no end if one could be found at such an ungodly hour.

"Is that altogether necessary?" he said, pointing to the bindings at Robey's wrist.

"He's a prisoner-spy," the soldier said and tugged open the blue jacket to show gray.

"Please," the major said. "Untie the young man. We'll just have to take our chances." Then, to the young officer with the leather book, he expressed the sentiment that someday this war would be over and when it was they would all have to live with each other once again.

The woman directed her maid to immediately kill a chicken and broil it for the good major. She then told the major a fire had been built in the library and he should sit by the fire and warm himself as the night outside was turning cool and wet.

"It's spring nights like this that the cold can deceive you the most," she said, to which he agreed. She then told him he should rest himself as the train was running late but should be along shortly, and when it finally arrived he would surely be busy with the off loading.

The major looked at his watch in the palm of his hand and asked her how she knew his train was late.

"I have ears to hear with," she tried in her most alluring manner.

"Yes. Yes you do," he said. He found the young officer's eyes with his own and communicated reprimand. He told the woman not to concern herself with the train. It was his business to know when the train would arrive as it was his train and then he disappeared through a doorway deeper into the house's interior.

It wasn't long before the young officer with the leather book came to the parlor and indicated they were to follow him. As he stood, Robey cut his eyes to the girl, but she sat quietly, her hands folded in her lap, her vision cast in the direction of a tall window.

The young officer led them down a long lamplit hallway, smoky and orange and hung with family portraits set in ornate gilded frames to a room that fronted the square. Inside the room, a gallery walled with books, was a fireplace and the major straddling a wooden chair close to the crackling wood. He'd removed his damp jacket. His collar was unbuttoned and he sat as one who wanted proximity to the fire. His arms were hung off the chair back and in one hand he held a glass of amber-colored whiskey. He was teetering back and forth, letting himself onto the front legs of his chair and then the hind legs and closer to the flames where he was sweating and seemed to feel the strange need to do so.

In the doorway stood the old woman whispering to a much younger version of herself. She too wore pearls and a tightly bodiced peach dress with ample skirts. The woman's daughter, Robey concluded. Though they were whispering about the major, she seemed intent on another individual in the room, a black-haired cavalry officer.

"Too old," the woman was saying, and Robey could see how right she was in her observation. However alert and vital the major at first had seemed, in repose he showed himself to be too old to be in a uniform, his smiling head perched on its stiff collar, his purple-spotted hands hanging from his shirt cuffs, tufts of white hair similar to his eyebrows rimming his red shell-like ears. His face, though elderly and care-worn, was the man's face returning, as some men's faces do, to its original boyish likeness.

"He's a very important man," the daughter was saying, impressed with the major, his staff and attendant military trappings.

"Not down here he ain't," the old woman said, her voice betraying the truth and depth of her bitterness.

The major turned on the blabbing women and then smiled broadly to let them know he could hear their imprudent hall-way whisperings. They fluttered at how unsettled they were made by the gaze of his clear blue eyes and the knowledge they'd been found out.

"It's a young heart that beats in this old body," he told their

fleeing backs, and then he saw Robey and his guard and gestured with the wave of his hand that they should enter.

When they made their way into the room, there were two
tall guards standing inside the entry and another officer
lounging crossways in a reclined chair, his legs slung over
an arm. This officer wore the gold braids of the cavalry and
of all the men in the room seemed most secure in himself.
His hair was black and glistened with oil, as did his tall shiny
boots. He held a gold-framed hand mirror and scissors and
was trimming his elaborate waxed moustache. On the floor
beside him was a half-eaten bowl of buttered popcorn.

"I am tired to death," the major said to no one in particular, and turned back to the fire that was reddening his face.

The guards took this as a sign, for they smiled and shifted
to stand at their ease again. Then propping his arms on the
chair back, the major turned his eyes on Robey and said to
his guard, "Who is this young man you have for me and why
so urgent?"

"He's a peculiar one," the soldier said, prodding him forward with the stock of his rifle. "I sketch him a spy."

The cavalry officer could not contain his laughter. "A spy,"
he scoffed, and caught his image laughing again in the mirror glass.

"Don't be shy," the major said to Robey. "Can I offer you a
drink on this wet night?"

"It might help warm me up some," Robey said, and gave
off a shiver at the suggestion of how chilled and thirsty he
might be.

"He talks," the guard said, as if it were a suspicion confirmed.

"He talks," the cavalry officer mimicked, and then made a sound of disgust in his throat.

"Has he not talked before?" the major asked.

"Nope, not a word come from him."

"Then how do we know he is a spy?" the reclining cavalry officer said, without breaking concentration with his mirror.

"Are you a spy, son?" the major asked, looking again at the watch he held cupped in his hands.

"No sir," Robey said.

The major continued to ask questions as if his aim was to ask a certain number in the shortest amount of time and the substance of the answers did not much matter to him.

Robey didn't know how to reply after the first question and so he clasped one hand in the other and said little more.

The major looked up from his watch and, seemingly taken by Robey's face, caught his eye and smiled and would not let go the stare. The major held the stare, looking him straight in the eyes and Robey met his gaze and would not turn away and before long it was as if neither one of them was located in the room. It was no longer night or day and neither of them was in the environment of war. The major was somewhere else—another place and another time and that's where he was seeing Robey.

"Have you had any formal schooling?" the major softly asked, and when Robey did not answer he explained how before the war he'd been a schoolmaster in Connecticut and he had taught boys much his own age and how much it saddened him to now see them in uniforms and carrying swords and rifles and slaughtered in battle.

Robey thought for a moment as to what he might say to

this man who was experiencing an occasion remote and ruminative. He folded his shoulders and out of respect he looked down at the worn carpet beneath his feet. The cuffs were worn from his trousers and the fabric ragged and thready. He'd not realized how tattered he'd become and had the odd thought it was time to find another pair of trousers. He was learning that fear was like danger and passed by those who faced up to it. The straying thought lingered: new trousers. He thought this day would not be his end. He decided he feared nothing from these men and looked up. He looked straight at the major, unmoved by the old man's rheumy solicitation.

"Well," the major said, draining his whiskey glass and clumsily setting it to clatter on the stone floor of the hearth. "So be it. What do you have to say for yourself? Nothing at all?"

"I am searching for my pap," he said.

"He is a liar," the soldier bawled, and to this the major shrugged, still holding his gaze as he let the watch dangle on its short fob.

"Son?" the major said.

"I am to find my pap and bring him back to his home." His voice became no more than a whisper on his lips when he said, "I were shot right here in the head and my horse were stole from me."

"The bastards," said the cavalry officer trimming his moustache. "They'll take the eyeballs right out of your face."

Again the soldier guarding him called him a liar and the major informed the soldier that he was no longer needed. Disgusted and long since tired of the duty he'd assumed, he shouldered his rifle and stamped out of the room.

"Sit down," the major said, pocketing his watch. "Let's have a chat."

"It is the truth," Robey whispered without moving.

"You wouldn't be pulling my leg?"

"No sir."

"Tell me what happened."

"A tiny little fellow back down the road. He was swum with skin fleas and dressed in women's clothes he stole'd off a woman he killed. He shot me here in the head," he gestured, "and stol'd my horse. It was a very fine horse black as coal."

"By gawd, that's the boy's horse," the major shouted, and punched his fist into the palm of his open hand. "We found the fellow who stole your horse. He's in the hoosegow as we speak. He's one of ours and I assure you in no uncertain terms, he will be taken care of."

"How do we know it's his horse?" demanded the cavalry officer. The mention of the horse had caused him to set aside his mirror and scissors and lunge to his feet. As he spoke he cut the air with his hand.

"No," the major said, wagging a finger at the cavalry officer. "The boy speaks the truth and you, sir, are working on my last nerve. I think you like that ill-tempered horse better than you like people. The story is impossible to contrive. You will give the boy his horse."

"I will not."

"You will give back to the boy his god damn horse and you will do it now and that will be the end of the matter."

What was between the major and the cavalry office was personal and what had been smoldering now burned hotly. The major was clearly pleased with his display of anger in command. In a sulk the cavalry officer shook down his trouser legs and, hands clasped behind him, looked to the ceiling as if in supplication. After enough delay to communicate that the final decision was his and his alone he left through the door, the guards snickering at his back with full intention that he should hear them.

"I will write you a letter," the major said, "explaining your purpose and signed by me."

"I had a letter before this happened," Robey explained, "and it didn't do much good."

"It is the best I can do," the major told him, and when he gestured the young officer with the leather book of papers stepped forward, opened its cover, and laid out a clean sheet of paper, a pen, and bottle of ink on a stand. He then held the book as a surface to write while the major dipped the pen and in flourishing script stated Robey's business and his stewardship of the coal black horse. He periodically cursed as ink spurted from the scratching pen and from time to time raised his hands that it should be blotted.

"Just sit quiet, son," the major said to the book of papers as he wrote. "It won't be long and you'll be on your way."

While they were still sitting by the fire the woman of the house ushered in a man and his wife. She said outside it had begun a plague of rain and the parlor was full and asked if the major would agree to sharing the fire with these itinerants, and to this he consented.

"Will my broiled chicken be much longer?" the major asked as he continued to write.

"There is a terrible downdraft," the woman said, and then told him the fire was being fickle, but it was apparent that she had completely forgotten about the major's chicken.

She sat the man and his wife by the door where they maintained themselves in mute sadness. The man was bare-legged and carried a large bundle on his back. The woman carried an infant less than a year old, wrapped in a blanket, and the presence of the baby seemed to soften the major. Clearly, he himself was a fond father and Robey could only conclude it'd been a long time since he'd seen his children.

The child was placid in the woman's arms, making not a sound, and still she spoke to it, saying its name. They were both wet and chilled and about them was the mystery and awe of hunger. The major ordered for them a mug of hot cider, then entered into conversation with them while he continued to improve his letter on Robey's behalf.

The man stood when the major addressed him and listened like he was used to it. The man told how he was by trade a weaver and his wife was the great-granddaughter of the Reverend Mr. Lamb, formerly minister of Baskenridge Church. They had been burned out and were traveling west to escape the hostilities.

"You travel a long way from home," the major said.

"Yes sir."

"Is Emily your daughter's name?" the major asked, glancing down at the watch he again palmed in his hand as the young officer folded and enveloped Robey's letter of safe passage.

"It is," the weaver said.

"It's a beautiful name," the major said. "I also have an Emily."

"God bless you," the woman said.

"Satan especially hates women," the major said with an exaggerated wink of his eye.

He then took out a purse and gave the woman a silver dollar, telling her it was for the infant child, which overcame them both with gratitude. He called to the maid and ordered for them coffee, bread, butter, and honey, if there was any to be had. He then crossed the room and pulled back the curtains to let his knee rest on the sill and peer out at the street.

"Why haven't you joined up to fight for your country?" he asked the weaver, still staring out the window.

"They won't take me," the weaver said.

"Why not?"

"I have a black heart."

"Oh, Christ," a sentry mumbled, letting the butt of his rifle knock on the floorboards.

"What is it that constitutes a black heart?" the major asked, without the least interest and as if in reply came the haunting banshee wail of an oncoming train whistle.

"He has a mind disorder," his wife said with some panic in her voice.

Then came another long blast from the quills and the sound of exploding exhaust. The men in the room came to life as if from a long rest. Then was the sound of the engine's volcanic eruptions bouncing off the hillsides and splitting the wet night with their echoes, with great back blasts of soot, as the engine hammered up the last grade and began its run into town.

At that moment the front door flung open and a soldier yelled down the long hallway, "The train is coming," and the sound through the smoky and orange lamplight, past the portraits set in gilded frames was raw sound in its coming from some far-off place, booming through the streets and entering the house. The major turned on his heels and made for the open door, his guards following close behind with his coat and sword.

Robey waited expectantly, but they seemed to have no more concern with him. The woman carried her baby to the window to look out, but she could not see so she unlatched the window and let it swing open. She called out the arrival of the train and when she left the window's opening the drapes followed her on a wind that would not let them down. The sound increased and the room was washed in a sweep of white light, and he thought it would be a good time to slip away to reunite with the coal black horse. But something was wrong. He felt it before he knew it and then he knew it.

"Don't you go out there," the bare-legged weaver hissed at him, hunching at the window to see into the night.

"You stay here, boy," the woman said, shifting the baby from one arm to the next and sliding a revolver from the blanket's folds.

Still, he went down the hall to the open door where the old woman was fingering her pearls as she and her maid stood looking off in the direction of the train yard and the major and his guards mounting into their saddles and departing on horseback.

"Don't you go down there," the woman warned, and she reached for his collar to hold him back as he passed her by. He could feel her crabbed fingers at his neck and dragging across his shoulder as he slipped her grasp.

Already he was leaving through the open doorway and into the chaos of horses and teamsters, officers yelling out orders and cavalry dashing over the cobblestoned street. As he passed through the streets he detected the townspeople watching from behind their fallen drapes and from between the slats of their shuttered windows. Men broke from doorways still stepping into their boots and dragging their suspenders over their shoulders, their shirttails flagging behind them.

He didn't know why, but he crossed the square and walked the street in the clear direction of the glistening engine, its rods slowly rising and falling. Shotgun blasts of steam filled the black vault of the night. Frightened horses were rearing in harness and had to be quieted. A shaft of white light still bayed from the tinplate reflector, splitting the wet darkness as white carmine-tinted plumes swept past the reflected light.

A cavalryman yelled at him and he jumped back as the horse and rider surged over the spot where he had just stood. Inside the light was visible the red star of the headlamp while the iron clapper continued its tolling on the bronze walls of the bell, as if calling to him again and then again: come see what you have never seen before in your young life.

Robey gazed at the shining steel and copper of the engine that pulsed before him. A red line bordered in gold made a long stripe down its wet glistening barrel. The black-faced men were slowly being herded forward, treading warily, as if they feared they would be fed into the very noise of the engine.

The doors of the boxcars banged open and lanterns were lit inside the cars and they became incandescent and shown from within as the men collected forward and began handling the boxes and crates from the cars' interiors and into the wagons. The black skin of their raised arms was wet and silvery in the light and their faces streaked as if they were crying silent end-less tears. A red mouth would open or the light would catch the white of an eye, and this would cause a soldier to shift and raise his rifle and yell and then another soldier would yell and the yelling would erupt down the line.

He turned away and it was then, through a white blast of steam issuing from the cylinder cock, that he saw webbed in the sweeping steel slats of the low pilot the torn and masticated head of the bay horse, its eyes huge and pearly and fixed on the distance forever. He turned over inside himself and felt his jaw fixing and reminded himself of hatred and how anger was more useful than despair. But still that a horse should receive such an outcome, even in death. Then the strangest feeling came into him as he marveled at how powerful the machine and the way it'd cleaned the bay horse's head from the rest of its body. He found his breath again and thought to find the coal black horse, a revolver, the infested little man who shot him so cold-bloodedly.

Then a soldier screamed, God almighty, and fell and he could hear a sound coming from the walls and cobbles like hot spattering grease. Then, beside his ear, he heard the crying sound the air makes when it splits. Then another soldier was toppled and then a rider hove up and the word went out that a large force had struck the pickets and they'd been drove in. Then came the first of the pickets pouring over the river, the rail cut and in from the countryside, and in the same moment was begun the screaming sound of artillery in the night and in stark detail. It was as if the whole world about him was suddenly flying apart.

9

From out of the darkness continued a coruscating gunfire. Spent bullets were flattening on stone walls and dropping to the cobbles below where they hissed in the puddled water, or whining through the leaves of dogwood and cutting the green needled trees and falling to the street like elements of heavy rain. He saw a young soldier boy struck in the hand from a great distance and the force of the bullet seemed to fling the hand from his body and spin him in place until he fell down in the street to dumbly stare at his hand, as if an appendage newly attached and sourced with a baffling pain.

The horses standing in harness held their heads high as their lathered flanks heaved with every breath. They danced and trod heavily and then they too began to fall onto their haunches and sides but not before eight or ten bullets found their wet-sleeked hides, their withers, their long necks, their ribs, their croup, their powerful beating hearts. It was never the intention to kill the horses, but that was how thick and crossed the fire was in those first minutes of chaos.

He could see a cannonball striking sparks as it bounded over the rounded cobbles and then slowing and gently rolling his way. He jumped aside, but another soldier, his gaping mouth still gobbed white with a paste of crackers and cheese, held up his rifle as if stepping into water and put his foot out to stop the cannonball and in an instant his foot was gone and blood was gushing out the stumped end of his leg onto the street where his blood showed like red glass in wet sunlight. A second cannonball blew a soldier's head clean off and continued on to smash another man to death. The headless soldier walked three more paces before falling to the street where his dead body shook fishlike before extinguishing.

Robey lifted on his toes to damp the tremors circuiting the ground and a shock of fear went through him and it was like candied syrup running the lengths of his extremities. His belly swooped low and dashed at his pelvis where it fluttered. This night was war. The falling rain was war. The clipped moon was war. The earth where they stood and the sky they stood under was war. He had to fasten his mind to stave off the urge to piss himself and when the urge passed he armed himself with a dead man's revolver and then a second one he jammed in his belt. He determined, as if it were his prerogative to do so, that he would not be shot again by any man on either side of that small earth if he could shoot the bastard first. War would not kill him.

Horses reared and shrieked as the din of noise rose again and then surpassed itself. They kicked over the traces and kicking out with their hooves became entangled. A jack, braying and honking, plunged across the square, its ears swept back and its tail straight up in the air, a muleteer running behind, slipping and falling with broken leads still in his hands. Streamers of blood flowed from its nostrils, breaking and flattening and spattering its hide. It ran headlong through an iron fence and into a stone wall where it broke its neck and crumpled in a flower bed. Another soldier, his ribs blown out by an exploding shell, was revealed to him in lantern light, his throbbing heart, and he spoke on in delirium of a particular woman before he too expired.

Sparks flew from minié balls and grapeshot that hit stones in the hard gravel yards. The major, now mounted and crying out a babel of orders, rode up in a flurry of lather and sweat and stopped where he stood, and he could feel the fling of heat from the horse, panting and about to drop as it skittered to keep its tangled feet under it.

"Get down," the major yelled at him, and when someone pushed him from behind he scurried for cover in the wet grass behind a spiked wrought-iron fence.

Sharpshooters were now picking off the teamsters, the soldiers in the train yard and the soldiers in the tight confines of the streets, their flesh blurred by bullets. The major screamed out in anguish as a bullet passed through his black boot and entered his horse. A surgeon approached, dragged the boot from his leg and insisted upon immediate amputation, but the major kept him at bay with his drawn revolver, and the surgeon bound the wound while the major stayed in the saddle and continued his steady contribution of incoherent orders. Another bullet struck his wrist and his gauntlet filled with blood before he let it slip from his hand and slap to the ground where it lay red and bloated.

Then, from back a lane unlit beyond the great fountained square, came the long dense sensation that comes in advance of a great force marshaling. Then there was the force itself and that alone was fearsome and powerful to witness and then he heard the officer's command and the sound of slotted steel swords clearing their scabbards.

"Form fours! Draw sabers! Charge!"

Then came a sudden hurtling through space and behind it were the raiders materialized on horseback, kiting through the hedges and emerging from the alleys and gathering into the parallel streets where they charged like the bore from a burst dam, and then they were in their midst and abrupt explosions were erupting from the ends of their arms. Horses screamed and fell with groaning exhalations. A gush of blood spewed from another's mouth as it whirled on its hind feet and bolted. A blade flashed and a hand was cut off at the wrist. Another flashed and a man's head was nearly severed from his body and ropes of arterial blood tapped into the night's darkness.

There were now a hundred horses in the street, rearing on their hind legs, churning through the smoke and fire, the drizzle and blood. One soldier dropped his rifle and raised his hands and he was shot dead. Men were sitting up trying to staunch their own bleeding chests. A horse sat on its tail, both hind legs broken beneath it. With their swords the raiders slashed the gray canvas that covered the wagons and killed all who were revealed inside.

From broken windows in the upper stories, soldiers continued to fire and when hit they collapsed where they stood, falling to the floor or tumbling out the window to the ground below.

The major fought on, receiving saber cuts to the head and arms. His horse's feet pounded the air at Robey's face. The major grabbed a double-barreled shotgun from one who would shoot him and shot the man with his own load and then shot another and in short order he cut a third by the throat.

"Close up," he cried ferociously. "By God, close up."

But battles are determined by the soldiers fighting them and not orders from the top. The major was sitting bolt upright in the saddle when a minié ball came singing through the air and passed into his head and then he was dead and falling. The palings of the fence spit into his side and he was held there, stopped in his abrupt descent, his body pierced with black iron and dangling aloft like a great speared fish. His white face went blood red and gently came to rest in Robey's lap where he sat on the ground. His head still smoked where he'd been shot and his eyes were mere glass as they'd had their last flickering before his body fell.

Then it was over. And the air was possessed of an unnatural silence, but it was a silence that did not last long before it was replaced with hissing and roaring, with moans and screams. The enduring sound beneath sound. The silence had lasted for as long as it took the listening mind to return from where it had sought refuge from the gun's detonations to the timeless human sounds of pain and expiration.

On the ground around him came the moans and the sibilant cries of the wounded and dying men, the men stranded at the simple ends of lives. Horses had broken loose, and riderless they galloped about like the charge of a strange maneuvering ghost cavalry. He wondered what you did when a man shot in the stomach cried for water and you didn't have any water to give him. He stumbled across the face of the young officer who carried the leather book. He sat crumpled, half upright, and stared mutely at the red bubbles frothing from a hole in his breast as if he were aware of watching his life floating from him, his comprehending mind understanding how soon it would be and his active mind helpless to do anything.

They dragged into the light of the lit fires the cavalry officer with the elaborate moustache whose hair was black and glistened with oil. He no longer wore the gold braids of the cavalry but was wearing civilian clothes instead. He had been wounded slipping out the back door of a house on his way to escape.

"Put him through," one of them said, his voice half lit with whiskey, unable to stop what had been started.

"He ain't hurtin' nobody."

"It's a ugly bull that never hurts anybody," the first one said, and drew his pistol and shot the officer in the forehead.

"He's dead," the second observed, bending down and dumbly peering at the body before stripping it of boots and spurs.

"He is indeed dead," the one said, and freely conceded the hell he was already destined for. He then congratulated himself on how consistently true his shot and rode away.

"He loves to kill them," the second one said to another.

What soldiers had not been killed or wounded were gathered into the train station and made to huddle on the floor where the mutilated and dying lay packed together. Those who had fled were taken after by raiders on horseback and for some minutes after the battle came the sound of single shots from deep in the night's gloom as the hunters found their prey.

The blood was already turning black as the peddlers reappeared and began hawking their wares to the customers newly arrived. The raiders hardly paused in their killing before they attacked the slat-sided army wagons, where they discovered bologna sausages, hardtack, and sponge cakes. They turned the muzzles of a cannon on the train engine and blasted holes in the boiler. The water jacket ruptured and steam geysered into the air. Another round went through the cylinder and still another destroyed the crank pin and the driving wheel as curtains of water rained down on the cross ties.

After the battle, it was not long before he could hear the clack of dice inside a cracker box and after the battle there was food: milk, butter, eggs, and chickens brought from their hiding places and into the kitchens and onto porches. Stoves were fed with wood and pots set to boil. Afterward, doors and windows were flung open and invitations to eat were extended, and from a chapel the mounting voice of a choir followed the building strains of a pipe organ.

He walked the streets in search of the coal black horse. He thought too he might see the girl. He ate while he wandered, crossing street after street, discarding chicken bones in the gutters as he walked, but he could find neither the horse nor the girl.

These men he now walked among carried a sudden fatal danger with them. They seemed without cares and seemed as capable of turning on each other and even their own selves as they were of killing their enemies. They wore low crowned, broad-brimmed hats. They were long-haired and unshaven and their overshirts were dirty with camp grease and fire smoke. Their gray trousers were black stained with saddle sweat and horse lather. They wore three and four Navy Colts in their belts and carried shotguns slung on their backs. Their faces were darkened with sun and gunpowder. They did not walk but loped the canted walk of traveling wolves.

"Murderers," the veiled old woman in pearls said to a passing raider wearing a gold cord wrapped around his black slouch hat.

"Just murderers, ma'am, every one of them," the raider said, without hesitating and without looking her way.

THAT NIGHT HE SPENT what passed for sleep in a shed while a dog nearby sent up an intermittent barking and howling. During his wanderings he had learned that a regular army, one he concluded to be his father's, had crossed back into the valley at Front Royal and when he inquired he learned he was just days behind. A voice in the night told the dog to shut up its yap, but it continued its noise until there was the sound of a single muffled shot and then there was silence. Morning was only hours away when he could no longer hold off the crush of sleep and later it was still dark when he awoke, and in that short time the raiders had departed. They had disappeared as silently as they had appeared.

The morning air was damp when he came to and a dense grimy river fog rolled in across the grain fields. While the rest of the town slept, he hurried through the compact streets under the colorless sky, the faint light of morning still on the river. The gutters were now dry of runoff, but the damp was running from the walls and fences as if it were spring's last thaw. A keen northeast wind was sweeping the stony streets and at each corner a hot wet draft struck his body and cut into him. He was well armed and past the want of hunger and thirst. His clothes were mildewed and rotting on his body, but that could wait. His ankle was swollen and ached to his leg and into his hip and he felt his thin body was down to nothing but muscle and bone, but he did not care.

In the train yard were the dead buildings and there were the boxcars and there was the engine and the twisted trucks and all were shrouded in the wet acrid smoke of their burning. The streets were strewn with debris and mottled with swatches and runs of cracking blackness and he knew they were the bloody stains of the fallen soldiers. He needed a horse and he found one, a big cream workhorse with knotted shoulders cropping a trampled kitchen garden. It still wore a collar and the last vestments of a broken harness draped from its neck and dragged on the ground. It was a wounded and sorry mount, one jaded and abandoned by the hostlers, but it was stout, clear-eyed, and of even breath.

He mounted the horse and beat its hind end and jabbed his heels into its sides. The cream horse remained obstinate and heavy as a log as it slowly understood its charge. He jerked the makeshift bridle he'd fashioned and swore and slowly the horse understood and began ahead. It crossed over the tracks, its wide hooves grating on the ballast of broken stone and gravel between the ties. On the other side was a deep ditch and instinctively the animal sat as they plunged into it, stood, and bounded up the other side. Then they were on the brambled and nettled waste ground beyond the station and cindered rail bed and the cream horse, encouraged and not finicky in the least, breasted through them.

Here the land settled to the river bottom and was bathed in runners of fog and mist, and the wind was now slicing over his head in hot gusts. The horse slowed and stepped gingerly as the ground disappeared in the gauze of whiteness below its chest. He kicked the horse, but still it stepped no more quickly for his efforts, picking its way over the rough and uneven ground. From the east came broad trails of pale silver presaging the advent of another day's light. Then rising to his nostrils in a sweep of dank air from the earth below came the sweet cloying smell of newly wrought death.

His craw surged and he tried to bend away as he retched a clear fluid, but it drenched his knee and pant leg and when he opened his eyes he could see revealed in the passing windows of tattered fog, the soldier with the thin beard and gold-rimmed eye glasses who'd taken him prisoner and then the kind old major surrounded by his guard. His face was gray and his large head seemingly misshapen in the bone plates. All about him were the men in blue where they'd been carted and strewn for burial and the sight of them was as eerie as drowned fish. They were dead and face up and their eyes were open, as if watching his departure, as if they'd momentarily paused in this low wet place to witness his leaving before resuming their own eternal travels. He understood if he had to be dead to keep his eyes open and not forget to do that because that was the habit of dead men.

As he left that dead ground he entered a forest on a path that the cream horse found and it wasn't long before he heard a whickering in the trees distant, and pulled up. The fog was so dense he could not see what was before him and he leaned forward and stretched his neck and waved his hand before his eyes as if fog could be sorted away.

The whickering came again and it was close and then he found its shape and he could see it was the coal black horse. It had been watching him as he rode in and now snorted and pawed the ground. It tossed its head and made a sound as if impatient and even castigating. In disbelief he called out to it and it tossed its head again and then beside it he saw two legs dangling from the round bottom of a white dress. On the ground beneath the feet was a straw hat and a parasol. It was the little goose man and he was hung by his broken neck. He'd been unhorsed in the fork of a low branch. His tongue was purple and swelled from his mouth and spread across his chin. His eyes bulged from his face like hen's eggs and he smelled from where he'd pissed and shat himself.

At first he thought to apologize to the horse and would have except for fear the horse would not accept his supplications. He slid from the back of the cream horse and his face stinging with tears of restraint, he spoke gently to the coal black horse as he led it away from the little man's hanging. They walked slowly at first and then he stopped and pulled himself into the saddle. Then he urged the horse on and it hesitated before responding as if to acknowledge that its rider had learned some valuable lesson and should now be rewarded for such.

They bore off from the river and struck the forest. They came to rails and crossed them and descended the other side. It was a gradual descent but a continual bed of rocks or large stones. In some places, the horse was at a loss how to proceed through the wild and dreary land but figured its path on the move and pursued it with abandon. Throughout the hilly land was a profusion of springs where the water came from beneath the limestone ground, clear and fresh. The timber grew large and the woods became crowded with underbrush and fallen trees and rocks, and more than once the coal black horse found passage that would have scraped him from its back had he not lifted his legs or bent low on its neck. But it did not matter. Nothing mattered as they traveled deeper into the North to intercept the army.

10

AYS LATER AS HE neared the wide flat river of his destination, where the army of his father was said to be, there were fresh rumors of a movement in a northeasterly direction and it was as if the eddies of seventy-five thousand men up and tramping the dusty roads could be felt in the very earth itself. He was only days behind the march when he turned in its direction, following its tremors.

Long afterward, he would remember how fifty miles away he heard the thunder of cannons echoing through the blue mountains, the reverberations of the bombardment that preceded, as he was to learn, the final charge of the fateful battle. The next afternoon, he rode through a drenching rainstorm that leeched the July landscape of all color and after dark he met the saturated vanguard of the gray retreating south.

Another storm cut loose in the morning, one that was more vicious, and in moments the tide of men and horses, the drovers and their herds of braying beeves he was traveling against, were forced by the deluge to wade through the deep cloying mud like hogs, the turning wheels clogging from spoke to felloe and locked in its hold skidded over the ground. Insensate, he was drawn against the tide of sutlers and ambulances, the carriages and caissons, the long parade of the hip-shot, the mud-spattered, the blood-dirty, and the slaughter-gutted, the wheeling army of the dead and the dying. For twenty miles they came against him and the coal black horse in a relentless tide and he rode on without hesitation through their broken and driven ranks. Their calls of foreboding and their hollowed silences were a testament to the great killing and dying that had taken place where they had departed. They had died on the battlefield and now they died by the road and they died in the road and those that did were ground to pulp from the rolling iron-shod wheels, the treading of horses' hooves, the tramp of so many barefoot men.

At the end of that road, it was as if evil had descended and taken up inside man and caused man to flail and step before the bullet and receive the bullet and receive the blade and man could not help but put up flesh as shield against metal. For man to enter those fields had been to give up all will but the will to kill, or be killed, and to survive those fields was somehow to be cheated of death. At the end of that road, he knew was his destination.

He did not call out his father's name as he moved against the retreat, did not ask of those sunken and glassy-eyed men where he could find his father. He did not want to intrude on their suffering, but more so he did not want to be heard or to be seen by them. He wanted to pass through their gabbled ranks as if he were not there and as if he were something of an essence and was capable of splitting time and walking the seams of place unknown and unseen. He had done such before, walking quietly through the place of deer or bear, walking up to a rabbit and taking it by the neck as it watched him come on. He simply knew he would find his father because he knew his father would be where he went to find him.

As he approached the town, everywhere the eye looked was the litter of war. There was paper torn from the cartridges rain-pasted to every surface, shreds of ripped clothing, blanket, and sack trodden into the ground. There were sprung watches, broken plates and shards of crockery. He saw a boot, and then he saw a boot with a foot inside, a sleeve and then an arm inside a sleeve, a glove and then a hand inside a glove. There were dead horses, splintered caissons, the litter of corn cob and the brass tubes of cannons seated in the earth with their white oak carriages staved and broken and the tubes of the cannons blackened and bulging and cracked. A white horse, its forelegs shot off, lay on its side calmly cropping the tufted and trampled rye.

The trees were made white and glistening as bone where they'd been peeled of their gnarled bark and whole men lay in rigid contorted shapes and some others lay as quiet and as peaceful in death as if they truly were asleep on the picnic ground.

In the deadened woods where the bullets had stormed and the air still crackled with the smell of heat, sharpshooters were hanging in the trees by their cinched leather belts. Their bodies were turned out and they occupied the air like great frozen birds intent on kill and in a flash their flights arrested. They hung dead and could not raise their bodies, but it was as if at any moment they would come to swift and fierce motion, and for anyone to pass under their bowers would mean certain death.

Those were but the small images where his mind could isolate what it found and save it into memory, for about the fields of milo maize were fifty thousand casualties, fifty thousand men who were killed, and wounded and missing from the roles. They were in parts and pieces. They were whole and seemingly unscathed and wandering about as the future dead while others were vapor or grease or but rags of flesh and pulverized bone. Strewn over the few hundred acres was everything a man carried inside and out. There were enough limbs and organs, heads and hands, ribs and feet to stitch together body after body and were only in need of thread and needle and a celestial seamstress.

Their blood, gummed and clotted, was beginning to draw flies in the wet air. They lay with their broken legs twisted and contorted so, to even unfold a man in the attempt to configure him as a man would be near impossible. It was a horrible scene to witness, replete with sorrowful pleadings for water and assistance, while the silent dead resided in strange repose, their stiffened arms reaching to embrace a heaven. He decided from that day forever after that there must live a heartless God to let such despair be visited on the earth, or as his father said, a God too tired and no longer capable of doing the work required of him.

In places there were swarms of movement, bodies still wriggling as if with souls attempting flight, but in these environs he knew even the souls had been killed and he knew this down inside himself, though he'd been told by his mother when the body dies the soul is immortal. Then a head lifted and a death drawn face caught his eye. It smiled and called a name his way, its eyes large with recognition. He approached, and when he leaned closer hands took hold of him and tried to claw out his eyes and he could do no other than boot the man's head to save himself, and he thought, In war even the dead will kill you.

He continued on afoot, walking from face to face, the coal

black horse following behind, stepping gently over the dead and not addled by the rank iron smell of cooling blood. In one field, he found a lineup of dead dressed in butternut uniforms. It was below the brow of a western ridge and their hands were tied behind their backs and a single bullet had passed through their brains. He didn't know what it was and could only figure they had tried to run from battle. One had a handkerchief tied over his mouth, perhaps to shut up his whimperings. He too was wounded mortally through the brain and they must have done it to keep him from hollering on the occasion of his imminent execution. Or maybe he'd gone mad. Or maybe he'd been wise. It didn't matter: he was dead.

His blood went hot and pulsed in his veins as he determined this was not to be feared for its horrible import but to be embraced for the knowledge it imparted. It was something to learn and to depend upon, another rule of the chaos. It disabused him even further of what he'd brought with him from the mountains. He saw that even they will kill you and if that is so, then anyone will kill you and he was relieved to know such and could plainly see how simple an equation war was becoming to him.

In one wood was collected a field of the dying, a long, sad row of men who lay on the bare ground, moaning and twitching fitfully, blubbering in wave and cadence. They were left wholly to themselves. These were men who'd been severely wounded through the head, some with both eyes shot out. They were all mortally wounded and had been put aside to die without hope as quickly and peacefully as they might.

Not far away from them was a long table where the surgeons worked from first sun to twilight and through the night, lopping off arms and legs with the quick gnawing strokes of their bone saws. Wagons carted away the bloody limbs and came back empty, wet, and glistening in the blaze of surrounding lanterns and again were loaded and hauled away.

It was as many and again and again into infinity as the most people he'd ever seen in one place—in his whole life together—and they were all limbed and dead and dying and their air smelled fetid as if an ocean shore captured for days at low tide, close and unmoving, quaked by no wind. He knew this was no brittle edge of the world he'd entered. This was the world itself.

There, in that wood, in the fleeting light of a declining watery sun was where he found his father. He was lying there, in that field of the dying men under a purple sky. He recognized him and he clasped his hand and his father stared into him with the look of an expectation at long last fulfilled.

A bullet had smashed into his father's cheek where it had left a black hole. It had then made a circuit of his cranium and exited out the back of his head. He could feel the ruptured path of broken bone the bullet had left as it coursed beneath his father's scalp before exiting through the wall of the parietal bone. When his father tried to speak, Robey encouraged him to remain silent. As they held to each other, all around them were the constant murmurations of the dying: giving orders, fighting, praying, calling out the names of women and children, gasping, gurgling, and throat breathing.

"I came as quick as I could," he said, fighting the panic that had seized his voice.

"It's a good thing it weren't any quicker," his father whispered.

"I tried hard," he said, his father's head on his lap.

"I know."

There was a low moan he could not contain cidering from deep inside his chest.

"Hush," he told his father. "Hush now."

The moan began to grow and overwhelm his body and take possession of him. He had no control over it because it was his heart and lungs and backbone and he fought hard to not fly away into the thousand pieces of a boy flung into the sky and through the air and down into the earth.

His face burned with what he had discovered at the end of the road. He could never have imagined what he found, could not confront how terrible his failure. His mind fled from him and his body ached from trying to keep it somewhere inside his body—his arms or legs or hands if not inside his skull. The feeling ran the ridges of his spine like a dragging knife-point. Then it passed and he was not panicked anymore.

11

WHEN HE FOUND his father in the field of the dying, he tucked his jacket under his bound head and found another jacket, a blue one with torn yellow piping, so as to move freely about the fields. For several hot days and wet nights to come, the departing troops would be parched by the sun and pelted by the heavy rain that washed the soil where the stains of battle did not run too deeply. The days: a relentless baking sun, which sets cloaks of steam and breeding flies to rise in the air.

That first morning he awoke before light and tied the lead of the coal black horse to his father's wrist and pinned the major's letter to his father's blanket. His father roused and under cover of the blanket he let Robey curl his fingers around pistol grips and only then, with the horse standing sentry, did he set out to forage for food and water.

As he wandered the fields, he thought himself to be in his ghost form, the died boy who lived with the dead and ministered to the dead. He was not yet dead, but was still young enough to not attract attention from the slowly gathering marshals who were intended to bring some order to the ravaged fields of the battle's aftermath. He foraged for what nourishment he could find to sustain his father and his fallen comrades. Inside the scattered haversacks were crocks of butter, mutton, veal, lard, and jars of sweet preserves. There were bottles of wine and oddly enough to be found were old bonnets, baby shoes, women's gaiters, feather pillows, silverware, and jewelry. He heard in the town there were cart loads of bread, but these were soon gone and in the days that followed no more was delivered.

There was every imaginable form of wound to be seen, horribly mutilated faces and men without arms or legs, and yet they were still alive and floundering in the mud like something left by a great swashing tide. Men drowned in the puddles where they lay for lack of an unbroken bone in their extremities by which they might turn themselves over to face the sky. At night they lay out upon the cold and wet earth, staring into the glowering darkness of the sky as they whispered their final prayers. While the fortunate were bedded on straw and hay, a blanket, an overcoat, most were stripped and being robbed and had nothing, not shoes or boots, not hat or coat or tunic or trousers.

In the first hours he wore a lady's kerchief around his face, wrapped layer upon layer and would let it slide down when he went back to his father's side but after a while he became used to the universal smell of death and gave up the kerchief and forever after was immune and not bothered by it again, the iron odor of blood outside the body, the living stink of the wounded, the peculiar smell of expiration and soul escape.

As he walked, there were to be seen dead men, surrounded by scraps of writing paper, who'd torn up their letters and the images of their betrothed they carried against their bodies, lest they come into the hands of some uncaring individual and be published in the Northern newspapers. The still living beckoned to him and they thrust their last pages into his hands and he carried the letters to keep them from the scavengers moving about the fields.

The scavengers came like flights of starving birds. They were collecting what tokens of affection they could find sewn inside pockets and talismans worn about the necks, for the soldiers carried into battle braids of hair, lockets, curios, and women's scarves. The scavengers moved like crows in the garden, skipping from one dead body to the next, furtively going through each pocket and lining to steal what single item they could find. They twisted rings off fingers and with their single prize they shamefully slunk away. These were intended as the anonymous memento mori of one of earth's great battles and were destined for a drawer, or a closet, some private museum, or to be sold as reliquies, ransomed to bereaved families. The more industrious collected blankets, harnesses, and rifles. They led off horses, cannon limbers, caissons, and even ambulances they would rebuild as milk trucks and forage wagons.

Sticking among the rocks and against trunks of trees were hair, brains, entrails, and shreds of human flesh cooking black in the heated air. There were men and horses swollen to twice their size, and in the days that followed he witnessed the shocking distension and protrusion of their eyeballs and he would eventually see them bursting open with the pressure of foul internal gases and vapors, their bloomings like horrible flowers exploding their petals and leaves and spewing them across the ground.

Grave diggers came to work, men hunched over their shovels and the earth they turned in plodding fashion in every place heaving the ground uneven. There were two he watched as they filled one grave with the turned earth of the next. He thought they must have been at it all night for how long the sweeping, lifted mound of rolled soil they'd already left in their wake. He watched them until they paused with fatigue and one of them hoisted a jug to his shoulder only to find it empty. He wasn't close enough to hear their exchange of words, but apparently it was an argument over the empty jug. One of them dropped his shovel and doubled his fists, whereupon the other lifted his shovel in the air and slammed him on his shoulder cuff. They closed in a hold and struggled against each other, while beneath their feet were dead men, their eyes white as milky glass, until finally the grave diggers fell among the dead where they did not move except for their breathing chests.

In a peach orchard, he came across young men gathering up the amputated limbs and filling wooden barrels with them. When he asked them what they were going to do with all that limbage, they said they were medical students and they were going to bury the barrels in the ground until the limbs had decomposed and then ship them to Washington to the medical college to use in their studies. Another team of students was boiling the flesh from the skeletons of the fallen gray soldiers, working diligently with paddles and hooks as the flames licked at the sides of the steaming black iron kettles.

There were two scavengers he followed that first day and studied for especially how they worked. Over the course of time he learned how they were unlike the others in that they were not interested in keepsake or memory or usefulness

but rather had a professional way about them. They arrived
with the same tools as those of the surgeon or mechanic. They
would wear carbide lamps to move about the field at night and
maintained a variety of disguises. They camped a safe ways off
and were not greedy for the accoutrements of war, and what
they did take of war's implements they were selective about the
pieces they stole. The two were searching for jewelry and certain personal items. They wanted anything with an inscription
or an address which they might then sell to loved ones back
home. They did not go through the pockets or the linings of
the dead but slit them with razors they wore in their sleeves to
be the quicker about their business. They carried iron shears
in their pockets for cutting off fingers to get rings and wielded
jawed pliers to remove gold from the mouth.

By that afternoon, the citizenry had begun arriving in
flocks and tramping out to tour the battlefield. They were old
fathers and mothers, brothers and sisters hunting for their
wounded and dead. The fields were strewn with rifles and
all manner of outfit, and these likewise were collected up as
trophies by the citizens and more than one of the innocent
and curious was killed by the accidental discharge of a rifle
still loaded and cocked.

Side businesses sprang up. Women were charged twenty
dollars to move a husband or a son from the ground into a
wooden box and onto a cart, and he took advantage of this
opportunity and his arms ached so for helping that day he
could not lift them from his sides. When the women tried to
pay him, he refused at first, but finally he relented, whatever
they wished to give, and accepted the few coins they left for
him on the ground for fear of touching his blood-slick and
fat-greased hands.

With the money he walked into town to buy water and a clean dressing for his father's head. He saw two women, one older and one younger. They were sitting in the open doorway of a gray stone house. By their doorstep, the syringa bushes were in bloom and white lilies had unfolded on bowed stems. He took their relationship to be that of mother and daughter. They were laughing as if nothing had happened and he could not help but smile at how happy they appeared in spite of their surroundings. He opened their gate and his throat parched, he called out to them for a sip of water.

"Water," the mother said. "You want water after what you did?"

He slowly shook his head. As hard as he tried he could not think what he had done.

"You can't tell?" she asked, and then answered her question for him. "You scared all the birds away and they won't ever come back." Both women laughed at this for how funny it was to them.

"A sip of water is five cents and by the glass is fifty cents," the younger woman called to him.

He held out his hand to show her the coins he possessed and she motioned for him to approach. He went to them along a path of red bricks lined with trampled yellow flowers. She was a blue-eyed strabismal woman with a high color in her vein-traced cheeks. She held her legs clasped in her arms, her chin hovering her knees. The older woman had a boiled look to her face, as if she'd been burned, but she wasn't burned. Sweat ran down the sides of her thin face and collected in the bones of her shoulders and chest. They each clutched a square of cloth to their face from which they inhaled deeply and between them sat a stoppered bottle of rose water. He held out the silver coins again and the younger woman indicated he should drop them in the berry pail at her feet. When he did, the older woman stood and disappeared inside the house.

"Bread?" he inquired.

"A loaf of bread cost two dollars," the younger woman said, growing impatient with his trade.

This money he also let drop into the hollow of the berry pail and this time when he did he leaned forward and looked down and saw it to be full of coins and greenbacks.

"You stay back there," she said sharply. "Don't get so near. Bring a loaf of bread," she called into the house.

The older woman returned with a glass of water and a loaf of bread less than the size of a muffin. She waved him off and when he stepped back to the gate she set them on the bricks in front of him. She then returned to the step and nodded him forward after she sat.

"Drink the water and go," she said. "And take that with you. You can't eat that here."

"Would you have some linen to bind a head?" he asked, after draining the water glass.

"Two dollars."

He paid her this money as well and taking the rolled material he left out the gate. Behind him, they resumed their private laughing, at what he did not understand.

Making his way back through the gathering crowds, he came upon a cemetery where a woman was digging a grave beside a file of dead men. Inside the wrought-iron gates the grass appeared blue and he was drawn to step inside and stand in that grass, and when he stood inside the fields of war beyond the fence appeared white in the bleaching sun.

Possessed by the orderliness of the place, he walked among

the riven stones of the cemetery. War had even been made upon the cemetery and in places the ground looked as if plowed. The tombstones were broken into fragments and graves had been turned up by plunging shells. The monuments had been toppled to provide cover for a time and so they were pocked and scarred by the scrape of bullets. The bodies slumped behind the stones had absorbed the bullets made of pure, hollow, soft lead, arriving to kill at a thousand yards, fracturing and shattering bones, blasting tissue, and causing large gaping wounds that draped like cut mouths in the sun.

He counted there to be thirty-four of the dead that she was burying and when he asked if he could help he learned she was six months pregnant, but she made no mention of a husband or father to the baby she carried.

"How did this happen," he asked, not quite sure what he meant, even as he was asking the question.

She looked at him oddly, her head cocked to one side as she leaned on her shovel.

"You are not from around here," she said.

"No ma'am."

"Why are you here?"

"My mother sent me to fetch home my pap."

"Did you find him?"

"He is over thar. I was to get water, but I drank it all myself. Then I paid for a bandage and I did not have any more money to buy water for this canteen."

"You can help if you want to," she said. "I will give to you water to take, or I'll just give you water and you can go."

"I have never had money before."

"Then it will give me pleasure to pay you in water."

For a time he helped the pregnant woman plant the dead. Their various causes of death were most apparent as the minié ball was a terrible, crippling, smashing invasion of the body, shattering and splitting bones like green twigs and extravasating blood in a volume of tissue about the path of its ferocious intention. The killing wounds were to the head, neck, chest, and abdomen. When the minié ball struck it flattened and tumbled, fissuring and comminuting bony structures. Shards of bone and broken teeth often flew from its path, wounding one body with the bones and teeth of another.

Most of the killed in the cemetery had received long-distance mortal head wounds in the lee of those signifying stones, as if the stones were waiting and would not be denied their purpose in life. Many had been shot in the left hand reaching up to slide the ramrod into their rifles.

He silently dug into the earth, his hip close to hers. Stray hairs floated about her tired face. She would tuck them away and they would come free again and she would stop to rearrange her hairpins. He thought of his mother and for the time he was a child-boy again and he was home and they were working in the kitchen garden, digging, planting, and hoeing, and soon he would share with the world the advent of an infant brother or sister.

When the hole was deep enough, together they would lift in a man and then beside that grave, they'd dig again, filling in that one with what they excavated from the next one. He worked his shovel hard so she might have that much less to do, but she dug steadily and held her own.

As darkness came on that first long day, he stood up from the new grave to grasp the next man and he saw that it was a boy his own age. His teeth were broken in his mouth and the bone cup for his hip must have been shattered because his leg was extended at an odd angle from his hip. Simultaneously, he felt horror and dignity for how young the boy was. The woman began silently to cry, the back of her hand at her mouth and he knew it was not so much for the young boy as it was for the little straw he was and the weight he added to her already heavy burden. Her chest caved and her shoulders shook and she wept quietly into her hands. He helped her to sit and stood by her side while the anguish passed through her like a steady racking wind.

"I am sorry," she said, daubing at her wet face and leaving it smudged with graveyard earth.

"He were a drummer boy," he said, bending to take the broken sticks from the boy's hand.

"Dear God," she said. "He was so young."

"Yes ma'am. Just a pony."

"You take his boots," she said, tears filling her eyes again.

"Ma'am?"

"I think you will need his boots."

They buried the drummer boy with the earth of a new grave and when they had completed the mound, he took up the broken drumsticks and slid them into the black dirt.

"That's enough for now," she said.

Then she led him to a stone house that stood nearby, its walls pocked with bullets. From a cistern she took a jar of milk and made him drink from it until his belly ached and then she filled his canteen with fresh water and made him also take a loaf of bread. She continued to apologize to him for reasons he did not understand. There was nothing he could determine that was her fault, nothing she could possibly have done wrong. She told him with conviction that people should be born twice: once as they are and once as they are not. He did not understand this either, but the way she said it convinced him it was true.

"Someone believes something that's wrong," she said, "and that person gets others to believe it too. And then everybody believes in the same mistake."

He asked her which mistake she was talking about and his question made her voice go cold to him. She told him he could just about take his pick if he wanted and then she warmed again and her voice pitied.

"You be careful," she said, her hand on his shoulder.

"Yes ma'am," he said, relieved that she had recovered herself.

"You will take your father home?"

"I promised my mother."

"A broken promise is worse than a broken bone."

"Yes ma'am."

It threatened to rain again as he made his departure, the dry lightning illuminating the faces of the unburied dead at the cemetery gates. He hastened back to his father to cover him with gum blankets he'd secured. His father was sleeping as a soft, insignificant rain began to fall, and was at peace and only woke when he tucked the blankets to his sides. The coal black horse shook out a muscle in its shoulder and blew. For the horse he'd found a feed bag full of oats and its contents he spilled out on the ground.

"Son," his father said, pleased to see him. "I should say I am feeling a little puny tonight."

His father smiled up at him as he lifted his head so that he might have a sip from the canteen. He tipped the canteen and let the water leak into his father's mouth. He then let his father's head back down to rest on the jacket his mother had sewn.

"The church pews is full of wounded men," he told his father, "and outside the window is a wagon where they toss the arms and legs. They say they've run out of chloroform and sharp saws there's so many. Near twenty thousand."

"Oh, it was a big thing," his father said of the late fought battle. "Biggest thing you ever saw in your life. Some of the boys had to get drunk three times just to get through it."

"There's rows and rows of 'em laying dead," he said, trying to understand what he'd seen.

"When they advance, they are afraid and they want to be close to each other," his father told him. "They want to feel the cloth of the next man, but they need to spread out."

"They need to spread out," he said, repeating the words to himself.

"It was a terrible event," his father said. "It was as if whole brigades disappeared in a cloud of smoke."

"I have a clean bandage."

"Yes. The bandage should be changed. We will rest tonight and in the morning we will go home with a fresh bandage."

He touched at the crust of the bandage wrapped about his father's head. It was black and hard.

"Where was the sun today," his father asked. "Did it not come out from all the clouds?"

"It was sunny all day," he said, and it had been, hot and rainless.

"Not here," his father said, and he could only think it was the coal black horse who had walked the sun from east to west and made a shadow that shaded his father from its rays.

He cradled his father's shoulders in his lap and with a pocketknife he began cutting at the old bandage as gently as he could. The horse stopped its feeding as the bandage came away in chips as if it were tree bark and he could not tell what was skull bone or rotted bandage as it came away in his hands. He looked up to see the horse watching them with what seemed like mild curiosity while it ate.

"There is a law of nature," his father said, "that produces rain or snow after a great battle. It is the same in France and Germany. I knew your mother would endeavor to find me."

"She sent me when General Jackson died."

"I was there," his father said.

"When he were killed?"

"I was there," his father said.

As the bandage came away, so too came more patches of scalp and shards of bone and necrotic tissue. Revealed to him was the black hole bored into his father's cheek.

"That does itch not a little," his father said, fumbling a hand in the direction of his head but then giving up and letting it drop back to the ground. "Maybe another day for us and you will take me home to your mother."

"Yes," he said, and his throat constricted as he held the back of his father's macerated head and felt the maggots falling through his fingers and away into his lap.

His father gave off a convulsing shiver and then sighed and settled again, and it was as if another piece of him had died and departed and there was little hope of recovering it. He worked quickly, scraping lightly at the wound rot with the knife blade. He then bound the wound with the clean linen he'd bought from the two women earlier that day and lay down beside his father and held his broken and ravaged head.

"Mayhaps, when it gets a little later, you could find a cart and a pony. I would not suggest you steal for they are something we could return."

"I can do that," he said, and he thought, This is my father and I am his son and it brought him a degree of peace.

"Or maybe tomorrow night," his father said. "Another day's recuperation would make me stronger."

"Tomorrow," he said, and thought he might cry for the storm he felt in his face, but he didn't. "Now would be a good time to get you some sleep," he encouraged.

"Soon," his father said.

"Soon," he said.

That night he awoke to the sound of a shot and a man crying out. The night had brought no relief to the day's heat and now a gunshot. He sat up to see the shallow graves in the moonlight giving off a phosphorescent glow. It radiated from the fresh turned earth above the burial pits, and passing through the light of the glow he could see low-running, slab-sided hogs come to root out the dead bodies already inhumed. At the far end of the field of the dying came a scream and a scuffle and a cursing that awakened and traveled the length of the head wounded in a long mimic of moaning sound.

He took up a length of broken sword and went down the row until he came to a soldier propped up on one arm. He was gibbering and pointing in the distance with a revolver. His eyes, his nose, his lips, his face were shredded by shell fragments.

"It is my own leg," the soldier kept saying, again and again.

The soldier waved the barrel in the direction of a nearby feeding hog and he did not understand the full import of that until, plaintively, the soldier explained, it was his very own leg the hog was feeding on and in his mind he knew the leg was no longer attached to his body, but however he tried not to, he could feel the teeth of the gnawing hog.

"I can feel the pain as that hog gnaws at my shin," he cried, pointing the revolver into the darkness.

Beside the soldier was another, lying face upward taking breath in rattling snorts and blowing it out in sputters of froth which slid down his cheeks in a white cream, piling itself along one side of his neck and ear. A bullet had clipped a groove in his skull above his temple. From this opening his brain protruded in bosses dropping off to the ground in flakes and strings. Then he stopped breathing and then and there he was dead.

"Stay here," the soldier said. "Don't leave me. I cannot see."

"They are over there," Robey said, pointing at the hogs' flat shadows crossing in the darkness.

"I am blind," he said.

"My father," he said.

"Stay until I die so as I will not to be eaten alive by that hog. It won't be long now."

He did not want to leave his father's side, but still he took up the sword and for the next hour he guarded the field of the dying. Of all that he might wonder on, he wondered on why the blind soldier was blind.

"Why blind?" he whispered as he walked. "Why blind and still not dead."

He walked the fields length, turned smartly, and then returned to the soldier who'd endured the phantom pain, and
after several such circuits he was tired and impatient, so he
went into the field where the hogs were rooting and lay down
on the surface of the flat wet grass with the sword at his side.

He waited and finally one of the curious beasts came close
and nosed at him with its great tusked snout and when it did,
he brought the sword up swiftly and skewered it through the
neck. The animal screeched, and open-mouthed it lunged at
him as he twisted the blade sharply and hot blood flushed
from its neck and down his arm and it made no other sound
again. He slaughtered it where he killed it, taking what fresh
pork he could carry and leaving the rest for its own kind. In
the morning he would fry its bacon and fat which had been
nourished with the flesh and faces of dead soldiers and he
could not but think that when he fed them, he would be returning them unto themselves.

When he returned to the soldier who had endured the
phantom pain, he was going to tell him that maybe he was
blind because God thought he'd seen enough for one life, but
when he arrived at his side he found him to be dead. On his
chest was the revolver, a six-shot Remington. It was loaded
and he understood that the soldier had left it for him. He also
came to understand that he was finally finished with his be-
lieving in God.

12

THROUGHOUT THE NIGHT HE was restless and in the early-morning darkness he awoke to the silent movement of women. He sat up and without passage into wakefulness he was alert and saw them wandering from body to body in the field of the dead. They cried into handkerchiefs they'd scented with pennyroyal or peppermint oil. They were stark, tormented creatures with unpinned hair and bent shoulders, wandering in the dawn, kneeling beside bodies, and collapsing to the ground. He wanted to call out to them, to touch them, to be assured that he saw them and was not dreaming them.

He looked to the horse silently standing watch and sketched its face with his own sadness and drew strength from its passive and mannered distance. Surely the horse felt what he felt. Surely the horse knew what he knew. The women were sisters, or mothers, or lovers, he did not know. They wept and stumbled on and he wondered if they truly wanted to find the men they were looking for. He himself had found what he was looking for and wished he hadn't for how slender and proscribed hope was now.

When he awoke again it was in the morning and it was because someone was throwing pebbles at him. When he opened his eyes it was to see the girl. He knew it was her before he saw her, but still he closed his eyes and opened them again and she was still standing there.

She stood looking at him without moving, her body in black silhouette against the sun, and he shielded his eyes to see her the better. He rolled to his side and could see that she was looking at him queerly. She was wearing a plain black dress with the sleeves cuffed in white lace and he made out she was carrying a drum on her hip. She stood beside the coal black horse and in her black dress was as if she was of the horse, born of the horse, and the thin sliver of yellow light expanding between them was their separation completing itself.

She cocked her head and squinted at him, studying him in her mind. Some part of her knew him, but she was not sure and he felt compelled to tell her in what ways they were acquainted. How their paths had crossed. He was tempted to say, Yes, you know me, but he did not. He returned her look and the guilt of their history must have been written in his face.

"You thought I wouldn't recognize you," she finally said, her lip caught between her teeth. Her words held no accusation, but still he felt accused.

He stood and gathered himself and not knowing what else to do, he began walking away from her, but she followed him to the tree and then her voice was asking to his back, "Who are you?" And then her voice was rising and she was cursing him and saying, "You could have stopped him."

"I could not help," he said, turning to her sad and stricken face. "I had to find my father."

She stood very still, disbelieving him.

He fought for control of the sound in his voice that it not be weak or pleading. He'd done nothing to stop the man and however much he tried to tell himself that he'd not known what to do, the after-knowing, the knowing that follows experience, was burned into him and what he'd thought before was slight and weak and not worth remembering. He could not deny that he'd become bound to this girl that night in the fire-gutted house. He could not deny that it'd been in his power to stop the man.

"And did you?" she said.

"Did I what?"

"Find your father."

She had begun to cry and her tears were strangely wet and glistening as they streaked her dirty face. But she did not raise her hands to wipe them away. She stood in the black dress with the drum on her hip as if she were the one struck with accusation.

"Don't cry," he said, wanting to console her, but his attempt only made her the more angry and he felt as if anything he might say she would think was lame and stupid.

"It ain't me crying," she said. "It's my eyes."

"My pap is under this dying tree," he whispered, and pointed where the coal black horse stood watching them, making its long shadow in the light of the morning sun.

"What's your name," she said.

"Robey."

"Is that so?"

"Yes," he nodded.

"How old are you?"

"Fourteen."

"You have not been broken yet, but you will be and when it happens you will know what it was like for me. What he did to me a animal wouldn't do to another animal."

He wanted to tell her he'd been shot in the head and so had his father. He wanted to tell her he'd already been broken and he lived, but he knew his father would not be so fortunate. It was a thought he'd not yet allowed himself to have and felt something structured that he had depended upon fall apart inside him and it made his eyes burn.

"What's your name?" he said.

"Rachel," she said. "Like in the Genesis."

"How old are you," he said.

"Fifteen."

"People should be born twice," he said.

"I'd rather not be born a'tall," she said bitterly.

"How could he do that," he asked foolishly, and a look crossed her face as if he were the incredible questioner and he prepared himself for another tongue-lashing, but her anger was too great for her to sustain. Her body wavered and he wanted to suggest she sit in the shade and rest, but his mind was made too awkward by her presence and he could not cobble his thoughts into words that made half sense to him.

"He thinks he's above ever'one else," she said. They were words she'd had a long time to think about and decide upon in her struggle to understand. "He talks about turning over a new leaf, but he'll never change, not one bit. He carries snakes in his pocket and throws them at people. He claims he can't be killed."

Speaking the words had the effect of sending her back

inside herself. He wasn't there anymore. It was just her and these words she was fashioning to express the thoughts of her mind that could not explain or escape the memory of what had happened to her.

"Ever'one can be kilt," he said, and he waited for her to say more, but the girl named Rachel was now lost and confused, and however immediate and profound her surroundings she did not seem to know where she was. She lifted a hand and let the palm of it open, and that was the best she could do. He waited as she slowly made her return, looked at him, and sighed.

"We are lodged in that cow barn," she said, and then, "You can see the roof over yonder." She pointed across the hull of the battlefield and he could see the cornice of a roof, its dull surface flaring with muted sunlight.

She told him she wanted him to know.

She then stared in his direction, not focusing on anything, but weighing a thought in her mind. There was a long silence between them that neither felt the urge to break.

Then she told him she was tired and she needed to rest and turned and walked away.

THIS DAY BROUGHT MORE of the scavengers and more of the relatives and citizens and now there were the tourists arriving by train to be added to their numbers. The air was bone dry and the heat of that July day was relentless beneath a high blinding sun, and soon after their arrival they became a vomiting lot, fainting and puking on the ground beside the dead.

He walked among them with a shovel over one shoulder and canteen straps slung over the other, the hollow sound of the knocking canteens reminding him of his day's obligations. He wore the revolver tucked in the back of his trousers hidden behind his coattail and a knife in his new boots. He watched them as they went down on all fours like dogs and heaved their guts until their insides were empty and there was nothing more to heave. Then he'd move on, finding it increasingly difficult to extend sympathy or pity.

One old gentleman he encountered, wearing a sombrero hat and a short sleeveless cloak, was sitting on a large tricycle inside a circle of the dead and unburied and for no reason he stopped.

"Are you looking for anyone in particular, sir?" he asked.

"Thank God no," the old man said, "but please give to me a shovel and I will help you with this terrible work for it is awful and shameful. There is no one here to cover these poor boys with even leaves."

"They's grave diggers working," he assured the old man. "They'll be along shortly."

"The very birds would do that much for them if I did nothing and left them lying here so."

He felt no patience for the distress this old man was experiencing, so he gave him the shovel and walked on, securing another not far away. He too had been innocent. He too had believed.

Today as he walked, there was a second landmark that kept him oriented. The first had been the comb of trees where his father lay dying at the feet of the horse and now there was the cow barn where the girl named Rachel was lodged, the cornice of its roof, its dull surface. He thought of her there, still with the man and the woman. He trusted they would meet again, trusted their lives had crossed for reasons he did not yet understand. The thought seemed natural to him. He would see her again because he'd seen her before.

As the heat persisted, finding water to drink for the coal black horse and the men in the field of the dying had become a chore. When it rained the first night he had been able to collect rain water in gum blankets, but it had not rained in a while. He knew of a well where the owner had removed the crank handle to those who would use it except for those willing to pay a high fee and that morning he had worked up his resolve to shoot the man if he would not give up the handle to his well. So hot was the weather. So thirsty were the dying men.

By the time he arrived to do the deed, a provost marshal was there and had taken the handle from the well's owner. He was spinning it in his hand as he threatened him with arrest. However, if he should choose, he could file a claim and the federal government would pay him for use of his water. The provost then returned the handle to the well and posted an armed guard while the owner went to file the necessary papers for reimbursement. Robey was first to fill his canteens at the well and returned to his father who had not spoken since the night before.

"ALL ABOUT US," he said to his father with wonder, "there are niggers burying the officers."

"They followed them into battle," his father said.

"They cry a good bit. Some are old and some are young, but they all seem to cry a good bit."

Robey tipped the canteen and water ran into his father's

open mouth until he choked and it blew from his eyes and nose. His body was stiffened with an arrested fit of coughing and then he composed himself. He daubed at the beads of wetness on his father's face and neck and emerging from the corner of his eye and then let him drink again.

"Which ones cry the most," his father asked.

"I would say it were about even."

"When someone dies that you love it is a very hard thing. They were like brothers to those men who died to keep them in bondage. Who can figure out such a kinship?"

"I asked of one fellow, 'Where are you going, walking in that direction?' I reckoned the direction he was going to be south when he could have just as easily have walked north."

"What did he say?"

"He told me he had to go back home to where he lived. I asked him why and he said, 'I have to tell them what has happened here. I have to tell his momma.' So I gave him some bread I had and he told me his name were Moses. He seemed like a good enough fellow."

"He was a slave."

"He said he were slave of a captain, mortally wounded and not yet twenty-two year old. He buried him under an apple tree over there. He told me after the war he would come back and get him. 'Why would you do that?' I asked him."

"What did he say?"

"He said to me his momma will want me to."

"You have never seen such gruesome sights and you so young," his father said, and made a rattling cough.

He took his father's hand in his own and held it tightly to steady him and could still feel the strength in his father's returning grasp. He didn't tell his father what he'd seen on the road, the sight of the shackled slaves rounded up and herded south like cattle, the slave hunters in their garish dress, their plumes and cold-blooded horses, their hooves scuttling like crabs in the dust, the coiled whips lashed to their saddles.

"I helped some fellows today and they gave me a handful of coins."

"What for?"

"Over in the place with the big rocks. They were taking picture-photos of the dead and asked if I would help them and so I did."

"What'd you do?"

"I helped carry them where they wanted them to be for their picture-photos to be taken."

"It was good of you to help," his father said, but was so tired he knew their conversation was ending for now.

"I caught sight of those scavengers again. They'll surely come to no good if they keep going."

"You stay clear of them," his father warned, and the strength of his grasp made him know how strong he felt his imperative and he returned the grasp, strength for strength. They held like that until his father's grasp weakened and released.

Then his father said his name and then said to him, "Do you think you can make that kind of decision?"

His words were as if a veil had been lifted on the moment. Their lives were in balance and asking and considering this question they were stepping back from fear and hopelessness and emerging into prospect. They were a teaching father and a learning son, timeless in their existence, the father born into the son as is the grandfather and the father before him and all the way back to the first. The father's life is foreclosed and the son's life is continuing and as always, only the unknown privileging one state of being over the other.

"I don't know what to do," he said. "I feel like I have to do something."

"You've got to ration it out in your mind," his father said. "I will not be there to help you."

"Yes sir," he said. He then gently rolled his father onto his side and he added more letters from the dead at Gettysburg to thicken his father's mattress.

13

WHILE HIS FATHER SLEPT, he could not help but be drawn to where he anticipated the scavengers' next foray among the dead and dying soldiers. It was a place he knew well with a curious array of round boulders wedged beneath a ridge with a stream falling from a saddle and passing through to course the orchard fields. It was the place where he helped the photographer position the bodies and set their rifles to their shoulders as if just shot.

He slipped away and it was this deep rocky place he went to, far distant from the town where the hospitals had been sited. The ground there was gullied and barren, and the fitted boulders seemed tumbled into place and seated in the earth at improbable angles. Some were strewn and others were cropping from the earth and others of the boulders could not be understood for how they came to be there. For days the stream had run red through that place and still it was not clean, but brown and murky.

The ground there was too difficult for burial, too distant from the hospital tents, and besides, the dead in that place were from the South and so they still lay out on the field of battle where they'd fallen. The few yet living were gathered on a scattering of straw under a canopy and were tended by kind women and their children who came out from the town during the light of day and went back home in the evening before dark.

With all stealth he moved on to this place and stood high over it in the shadow of a boulder. He could not sort the scavengers from the boulders and the black trees. White vapors that rose from the earth drifted the land in slow tatters.

He moved slowly, ten paces at a time, and then waited and listened. He moved forward again and listened and then heard a high faint wailing cry he at first mistook for a night bird, but it was not. He glimpsed a light and went down flat in that dense place on the duff of the forest floor. As he did, another light that came from behind him swept the ground where he'd stood and pointed into a ravine before descending. He watched the light dodging in accordance with the gait of a running man who carried it and remembered the lay of terrain as it was momentarily sketched in light before it went to dark again in the trees.

The moving light went down into the deep ravine and converged with a second light.

"What the hell," an angry voice panted.

"What's the matter?"

"The bullet-hit son of a bitch bit me in the hand."

"Well, whack him. One good rap to the back of his head and he'll be dead as a doornail."

There was a pause and then he could hear the dull thud and crack of a flat object striking what he took to be head bone. He slowly crawled into the place where they were and suddenly he was on the periphery of the intersecting lights that came from the scavengers' heads and pooled on a fallen officer crumpled at their feet.

"Did you kill him?" the one said.

"How the hell do I know?" the other one said, holding a hatchet in one hand and nursing the side of his other hand.

"What's the matter with you?"

"I tol' you the son of a bitch bit me."

"Get it done, god damn it," the one side. "We have got to get out of here."

"I will do as I damn well please."

The one leaned over and poked at the officer laying at his feet. He hooked his fingers in the officer's nostrils and drew back his head until his mouth gaped open and filled with the yellow light that came from the head lamp. He then let go and the officer closed and groaned.

"Well," the one said, "I shall be very happy if you'd please get that gold plate out of his mouth."

The other one took the hatchet to the mouth of the officer for the sake of the gold plate it contained and to which a set of false teeth was attached. He raised it over his head and then it flashed down through the yellow light. With a single chop, he sliced through the side walls of the officer's mouth, separating the mandible from the maxilla and leaving the officer's mouth a gaping and bloody maw.

"He's a rascal, that one."

"I'd like to see him bite someone now," the one said.

"He will not bite again," the other said. He then reached down and drew a straight razor under the officer's mangled jaw and cut his throat. His razor hand dallied in the sully of gurgling blood and when it came to light it held the dripping gold plate.

He followed the two scavengers that night as they continued their bloody work and continued to follow them as they took what they'd stolen back to a redbrick house a half mile from the battlefield. It was no bigger than a one-room cottage, built of stone and roofed with tin. The doors and windows were missing. and the north side collapsed into rubble.

From outside the small house, they entered into a small shallow cellar, no more than four feet high, and from under the floor came a light and he could soon hear the wheeze of a bellows. He did not think to leave off. He did not ponder his father's question, could he make that kind of decision? He had no choice, but thoughts such as these never entered his mind. It was as if what he was doing had already been decided for him and to not question them was part of that decision.

The dim yellow light built beneath the floor and began to glow from the cracks in the foundation. He found an opening where the sill had rotted and closed in on it, crawling to the light on hands and knees. When he lay flat on his belly he could see into the cellar and he could see them and when he did, a nameless emotion passed through him. It was the mere wisp of a feeling and he was galvanized by it.

They sat cross-legged on a dirt floor, a light between them, as men have for thousands of years, but this light was a small forge and it heated a crucible and into the crucible they were feeding, one by one, the gold teeth and the wedding bands and the gold plate just taken from the mouth of the murdered officer. One after another they emptied their pockets of the gold tokens, sentiments, declarations, intentions, and cures they'd scavenged.

"I don't like killing," the one said, working the hand bellows. "But what else can you do?"

"It is done," the other said. "In the morning we will follow the army when it moves south. I've had my fill of this place. The smell of it could bend nails."

Robey studied them for a long time through the foundation wall and he was not appalled but intrigued by their methods. Behind him a horse snorted, and startled, he rolled away and reached for his revolver. Back in the trees was hobbled a long-legged roan and a second horse stood beside it, a white-faced chestnut tearing at leaves.

Down below, the men were not concerned as they'd not heard the anxious horse. They unstoppered a liquor bottle and passed it back and forth and smoked cigars, and when the metal was molten the one took up iron tongs and lifted the tiny crucible while the other pushed a sandbox forward, its insides just big enough to hold a deck of playing cards. The one with the tongs poured off the liquid metal and it formed a rectangular light more lustrous than the sun, more lustrous than any light he'd ever seen before.

The two continued their drinking and smoking their cigars while the yellow light cooled, but his mind never seemed to lose the memory of how brilliantly it glowed. With their bloody hands, they flicked at the dirt on their trousers, inspected their buttons, and straightened their lapels. He concluded their work was done for this evening.

"I say we go to Harrisburg tonight and take the train back to Philadelphia," the one said. "I say we got enough and we can't be hogs about it."

"Why not?" the other said. "Hogs get fat."

"Pigs get fat; hogs get slaughtered."

"I stand corrected."

In the light of the cooling forge and the hardening metal,

he could see the one to be a lynx-eyed man, the skin of his face scarred and pitted as if by fire or explosion. His ears were truncated and actually appeared to have been cropped. The other took up a hot glowing ember with the tongs, leaned into it, and lit another cigar.

"They are backed up on the Potomac as we speak," the other said.

"Why are they there?" the one asked. "That ain't very smart."

"The river is too high for them to cross," the other said. He savored his cigar, rolling it in his fingertips, dipping the mouth end into the liquor bottle and sucking on it.

"That could be the end?"

"That is why we are not going to Philadelphia."

"I believe we should saddle the horses," the one said, "and get out of here this very night."

"I believe," the other said, "I will saddle the horses and I will be pointing them south. We aren't done yet by a long shot. There will be another battle at the river and we are going to be there when it is over."

The other one then stood and brushed his hands over the seat of his pants. He made his way up the incline in a scramble of rubble and disappeared into the thicket where the horses were hobbled.

Robey watched the one still sitting in the cellar, paring his nails with a penknife. He drew the revolver and cocked it, folding his body over the hammer to muffle the mechanical sound. He held it with the barrel straight up and could not recall how it was so very heavy to hold.

He then worked his way along the side of the stone foundation to where he could see the other one saddling the horses and feeding bits into their mouths. One of the animals suddenly tossed its head in the air. The man stepped back and cursed it and when it had quieted he punched it in the side, causing it to squat and then tremble and tread on the ground where it stood.

His work finished, the other man came back to the red-brick house. He spat in the dirt and took a step down into the cellar, ducking his head low. When his body filled the opening, closing off the light within, Robey stepped up beside him. He steadied the revolver on the bridge of his forearm, placed the tapered octagonal barrel at the man's ear, and pulled the trigger. The lead bullet traveled in an instant through his brain behind his eyes and left the vault of his head out his opposite ear. He collapsed and tumbled forward with the gun's explosion to sprawl across the legs of the one still sitting on the dirt floor.

The light below ground went out with a flare as he stepped back from the opening and cocked the revolver again. Then there was a long silence and he could hear the hissing embers, could hear his own breathing. He and the one still alive both knew there was no way out of that cellar except through the opening he now covered.

He waited, holding himself close to the stone of the foundation. If someone had heard the shot and came to investigate, he'd have time to slip away into the darkness, but it wasn't likely. Shots in the night in those fields were not uncommon occurrences. Nightly, there would be the lone banshee wails of a crazed echoing across the fields, then a shot, whether accidental or intentional, self-inflicted or inflicted on another, and then there would be silence again. Then another shot without preface or consequence, the fields armed and that dangerous. War still not satisfied. War still lurking.

"Who are you?" came the voice of the one from the black cellar. Acrid smoke from the smothered fire was beginning to wind in the air aboveground and mingle with the burned powder charge.

"Nobody you know," he said.

There was another long silence. The smell of burned hair came to his nostrils. Soon enough he'd know if someone was riding out to investigate the shot, but he doubted it.

"What do you want?" the one asked.

"I don't know yet. I just killed a man."

"You killed him all right."

"I was hoping to kill him," he said. He felt no knocking in his body nor in his chest or head or legs. His arms had not weakened but felt stronger and his resolve fastened.

"Well, that you did," the one said.

"He's dead, isn't he?"

"He couldn't get deader."

"It weren't hard to do."

"No. I'd say you have a regular talent."

He scanned the black line of the horizon for moving lights. He listened for the sound of horsemen. He could detect neither. Down below the ground there was only quiet.

"What's your name?"

"None of your business."

"Tell me your name, friend. Everyone's got a name."

"I don't want your mouth on my name."

"You've got mustard, I'll say that."

Again was the overwhelming silence. It held in the air as if the draping darkness was knit with yarns of glass.

"Parley?"

"What have you got?"

"I got a sack of gold down here hid up in the wall. Silver too. Do you want it? It's yours if you want it, friend."

"I hadn't really thought in that direction."

"Anyone hear that shot, the provost will come."

"If he does, I don't believe I will be the one they ketch."

"I have an idea."

"What?"

"I will throw you up these sacks."

"Suit yourself."

The sacks came up out of the darkness and fell to the ground where he could see their black shapes in the moonlight. He moved to retrieve them and when he did the scavenger in the cellar shot. The bullet missed him wide and he returned to the wall with the heavy sacks.

"Did I hit you?"

"No."

"I had to try."

"I 'spect that."

"I am sorry to've tried, but he was my brother."

"I didn't mean to kill no one's brother."

"Ah, he didn't know enough to come in out of the rain."

"He was a very bad fellow."

"Oh, he was all right, but you know what?"

"What?"

"You just can't polish a turd." The scavenger had a laugh at his own joke and then he said, "What are we to do now?"

"I think I am going to take your horses now and slip away from here."

"I appreciate that."

"I don't need your 'preciation."

"Then I will wait to come out if you do not mind."

"Suit yourself."

"Hey, boy. What if, say, that you just lay back there in the dark and shoot me when I come out?"

"I did not think of that."

"Boy?"

HEN HE RETURNED to his father's dying side, the coal black horse was restless and scolding. He muzzled it with his hands and it tossed its head and streamed slobber in the air when it smelled the scavengers' horses on him. He'd sold the roan and the chestnut to the man who owned the well. He woke him from his bed and told him it was best to send them upcountry for their health and the man understood and bought them without asking any questions.

He gentled the coal black horse and then he lay down on the warm ground with his head on his father's shoulder. He felt his father's arm lift and and his fingers fumbling until he hooked them to his belt. He lay quietly with his arm across his father's chest and his father's arm holding him. He felt the rise and fall of his father's breathing and he wished that sleep would overtake him and painlessly carry him from that place. He now knew that when he left, his father would remain.

He wondered would he remember all that he was experiencing. Would he remember these offenses he was committing, these days on the road, his search for his father. Memories as terrible and horrible as these would make it all the more important to forget them if he could, forget the names and faces, the land and the objects upon the land, forget everything he had learned of what there was to know about war.

"Where have you been," his father asked, without turning his head. He thought his father had found sleep, but he hadn't.

"To fetch a pony and cart," he lied.

His father gave off a cough that rattled from deep in his throat. There was an unmistakable smell to him and when he opened his eyes they were filled with vision and urgency and his breathing was elevated. Robey unwrapped himself from his holding arm and took his father into his arms.

"You have to know, son. What happened here was not enmity or brutality."

"Yes sir," he said. "I know. Rest now."

"This was not the raving mad. This was not for love or greed or ignorance. These are the well bred and the highly educated. This is humanity. This is mankind, son."

"Yes sir," he said, but he wondered, what about himself. Would he be able to face up to what he had done? Had his own actions not arisen from pride and righteousness?

"This is the nature of man and this is the world and if you are to live in it, you need to know what you have to do."

"Yes sir," he said, and he thought, Let the past go. Let it go. He thought, Be the judge inside your own mind and not let anyone else do that work. Determine for yourself because either side will kill you and those without a side will kill you and the women and children will kill you—all the instruments of war—and he had killed and he knew he would kill again without pause or hesitation or even thinking he had to before he did. In his bones he felt his lessons and once learned they would never be forgotten. They were lessons that could never be talked away or thought away. They were lessons as old as the history of the sun.

"You have to do what I think you did tonight," his father said.

"I know, sir."

"You know that I will not be leaving here when you go."

"I know."

"When you go, you are to travel south. Find Moxley and Yandell and Tom Allen and Little Sandy. They are with the battery on the Potomac, for the water will be too high to ford. They'll take you in. They will teach you. They'll take care of you. Tell them you are me. Say you are me."

"I am you," he said.

"It is so cold," his father said, and these were the first words he'd spoken that conveyed his pain and despair. "I don't be-lieve I have ever been this cold before and I have been cold before."

He gathered his father into his arms and held him. His father's head was a great putrid mess against his chest. He held on to him, and as he did he cared little for all that had happened and cared not at all for what might come in the hours and days yet to be. They were here and alive together no matter how short the time, no matter how fast the moment that was approaching, and when it arrived it would be less than an instant.

He held his father through the night and his father, already weak and frail, lost ground as the night bore on, but he did not let go his hold on him, as if it were possible that his holding could stave off the certainty of death. His father shivered and his body was cool to the touch and dry about the face and eyes. His father whispered something and he asked him please say it again and leaned in to hear better his voice.

"Where did you go tonight?" his father asked, his voice clear and strong again, as if recovery were a possibility.

"To find a pony and a cart to take you home."

"That's a good son, but I say I don't think I'll be leaving this field."

"I know."

"I think this is the last day of my life," he said, and then he made the abrupt sound of laughter halted. "Your mother won't like this one single bit. You'll have to tell her the news because I won't be able to."

He then clutched at his son's sleeve as he was seized by a great paroxysm that ran through his body more than once before leaving him alone. His breathing rasped and stopped and then it started again and he sighed. A heavy dew had fallen and the wetted field that stretched out before them beneath the moon was so like a wide path of white jewels on blue velvet.

"Oh," his father said, as if he were quietly relieved of another piece of his mortality.

He held his father's head in his lap with an arm across his chest. His father clutched that arm and would not let go his grasp. He felt his father's fingers curl and a strength transmitted.

"I am very tired," he said, and then another convulsion swept through his body, lifting him into the air as if a man fighting inside his dreams and then he was quiet again.

"It is time," he finally said.

"No sir. I don't think it is time yet."

"It is."

"No."

"It will be today."

"Not today, sir. Please."

"We will meet again in the old fields," his father said in his shallow fast breathing.

He knew his father's time was at hand, for he was assuredly on the path of the dying. He now knew everything died sooner or later and knew life meant little. He knew everything that was had been before. He knew the lives of men were mere and fragile wisps regardless of action, declaration, and self-opinion. He knew the earth was angry and evil was as alive as any man or woman. He knew life meant little to him, but this was his father's life.

"I am passing myself into you," his father said, "and you are already an old man." And then he said, "I will be coming."

However strange the metamorphosis of the son receiving the father into himself and in turn the son becoming the father, it was substantial and whole and he could feel it inside himself. He could feel it fastening its hold as the words were spoken. Then it was over and he was no longer a boy because his father was dead.

That night, when he cut a lock of his father's hair, he felt strangely calm and the reason was because he'd experienced the horror that left one so. When the experience began, he could not say. Was it a week ago or a month ago? How long he would be haunted by shadowy sadness he did not know. He wondered who could explain a world where human words and human bonds and human thoughts had so profoundly failed. He had the feeling of an inexorable tide rising up inside him. His eyes had seen so much death so near to him. He had the feeling he'd been just a hollow, hungry, empty boy held on the mountain waiting and waiting until the call came, until it was his turn to become one of these failed humans. But in the cradle of the mountain he'd never felt hollow or hungry or empty. He did not understand it, but he knew he was no longer afraid of death. He knew he no longer felt the half of something but felt whole and finished in his making.

15

H E WATCHED AS THE MOON slid into the woods. His father's grave lay beside him. In the last hours he'd wrapped his father in a gum blanket, folded its ends and bound them with twine. He then dug a deep grave, carried his father to its opening, and eased him inside, and around him he placed the sacks of gold and silver, the letters from the dead. He then returned the earth and replaced the sod and broadcast a scattering of twigs and branches that no one should ever find him until someday he might return and take him home.

Done with his work, he saddled and bridled the coal back horse and gathered his kit. He calculated he had but a few hours before sunrise cracked the horizon with its red. There would be heated air and a dense fog that would not burn off until late morning. That was if this day was like the day before it and when it came to weather, he reckoned it usually was.

He walked alone with the coal black horse across the open ground, its size and strength and equanimity becoming his own. He passed the ever-lengthening earthen mounds that had swept over the dead and swallowed them under. He re-membered where the bodies lay, the thrown-over, the back-arched, the headless, the drowned, the sundered, the men held tightly in each other's arms. He did not care that war should be so terrible. He'd had no choice and still he had chosen it. In one hand he held the reins and in the other he carried the capped and loaded six-shot Remington. It was his hand. It was his arm. Should he meet anyone this morning, he knew what he would do.

The cow barn was where she told him she would be. There was no stock, but there was oats and oat hay and straw, and implements were strewn about the ground. The walls had been shot through and at first the bullet holes were not apparent to him as in the darkness they were so like black knots in the rough pine boards. He picked his way through the rubbish and litter, scattered tools, milk cans, stools, buckets, harness, barrels, a dung cart, torn and broken and shattered, the hot sheen of a small dying campfire.

He found the man. He was in one of the stalls sleeping the sleep of the dead. His body was gray and slumped and his mouth sagged open with great exhausts of air and the guttural noise of his breathing. His broad chest moved slowly up and down, lifting the blanket that covered him and the stems of straw he'd tossed over himself in finding his sleepful repose.

He shook out an armful of feed for the horse and then a scoop of oats. The horse had become impatient and ready for flight. It had indulged him long enough. He promised soon and went back to the barn wall where he made his way along its splintered surface.

In the next stall was the blind woman. Her size had increased evermore since last he'd seen her. She lay on her side, her vast belly in front of her and her arms and head and legs made small by how huge with her belly she had become. Her face was misshapen and bespoke a grave and internal malady. What did the blind see in their sleep, he wondered. He remembered feeling kindly toward the woman before and even after what he'd witnessed in the shell of the burned-out house so many weeks ago, but now she was just another being in the shape of a human. She meant nothing to him and he knew if he allowed himself she would mean less than nothing.

He moved on and when the shadows shifted he could see her. She was in a last keyhole of moonlight that entered through a rent seam in the board wall. She lay under a blanket in a bed of straw in an empty stall. Her loose hair fell ragged across her bare arm. He patiently watched her sleep, waiting for her to awake and look in his direction.

Sensing a presence and still in sleep, she finally did stir and sat up and opened her eyes, the spears of moonlight cutting across her bare neck. She raised a hand that held a knife and slowly it turned with her wrist as if it were the knife turning her wrist and not her arm. She concentrated on the faint sensation that had awakened her. She knew something was outside the wall and close beside it in the darkness, and if it should come inside she would fight it to the death.

He watched her stand, a thin sliver of a girl in a dingy shift. Her hair fell past her shoulders and she held her crossed arms to her chest as if cold, the effect of which was to make the knife seem as if its blade was not attached to a handle but was a blade protruding from her body. She stared at the wall he was looking through but did not seem to understand that someone was actually on the other side. She stood erect and pulled her blanket over her shoulders. She stepped into the alleyway and after looking at the sleepers in their stalls she went outside where he met her and she was not startled to see him there but rather was as if she expected him. She let the knife slip from her hand, stepped close to him, and when she leaned in to whisper he could feel her warm sleeping breath on his face.

"You were watching me sleep," she said.

"Yes, I was."

"I felt you," she said, her eyes moving over his face, searching out what was wrong, as surely she knew something was.

"Me?"

"Yes. I felt you. I have been waiting for you."

"You knew I would come?"

"Why the long face?" she said, and then touched her fingers to her lips. Over his shoulder she could see the coal black horse and it was then she knew what it was that had brought him to her.

"My face ain't long," he said.

"I know why you came."

"Were you sleeping?" he said.

"I wouldn't call it sleep."

"My pap died," he said.

"I am sorry to hear of your loss," she said, and then she held open the blanket for him to walk into and he did so, without hesitation, and she closed the blanket and her arms around his shoulders. He let his face to her neck, let himself be held inside the blanket, let his body rest against hers. She smelled stale with sleep and sweat and days without bath water. She told him that everything dies and then, in time, it comes back. He felt her breath warm on his neck. Over their heads was the last slow wheel of the stars. Morning was only a few hours away and he had the sense it was a first morning, the morning of a beginning.

"He's not in this world no more," she said as if it were a relief and a blessing visited upon him.

"No," he said. "He ain't."

"Are you leaving?" she said.

In answer he nodded his head, his cheek to her neck.

"Take me with you," she said. "I have to leave too."

"Yes," he said.

Her arms tightened around his shoulders and he responded by drawing her body more closely to his own. He was here and he was leaving and he would take her with him. She asked that he wait a moment and when she returned she told him the man was asleep drunk. She then found for him a sweet potato buried in the ashes of the campfire. The skin was blackened and crisp, but inside the flesh was orange and still hot and steamed when he broke it open. Overcome with hunger, he could not help himself as he wolfed it down.

"Stay where you are," she said, pointing at him with her finger as if to fix him to the spot where he stood. When she returned this time she carried whatever kit she owned in a carpetbag and a small tight bundle of clothes tucked under her arm. She set these on the ground and then she held out a pair of scissors. He took the scissors from her, and when he did she bent at the waist, collected her hair in her hands, and held it from her scalp, telling him he should cut it away from her head.

The scissors were sharp. He cut through her hair and she threw it away and then prepared another skein for him to cut and he cut that one too. Then she stood and he worked his way around, cutting her hair until it was short and tight to her head. She ran her fingers through her scalp and told him it was good enough for now.

Then, standing with her back to him, she let the blanket fall and shed the dingy shift from her shoulders. Underneath the shift she was naked and the white skin of her body was blue in the night. Her body was thin and lithe and built with narrow hips. The bones in her long back were well defined, her shoulders, her ribs, the sunken shapes of her hind end, and there was a space between her legs made by how thinned and stick-like they were and he thought how much better he'd fared with his foraging than she had. But she moved with strength and sureness and without a single wasted gesture.

She wanted to leave as quickly as possible, she told him, and she intended to do just that.

She unrolled the bundle at her feet and it was a pair of boy's trousers wrapped around a linen shirt and a moleskin jacket. There was a wide leather belt and socks and shoes and a forage cap. Before she dressed in the clothes she turned to look at him, her hands on her hips. There was a boldness in her stance, her telling him to take his look if he was going to. It was as if she were challenging him with her body, as if she was asking unspoken questions: What will you do with me? How will you be?

He answered her when he did not move and did not look away. He then looked away to the east where the sun would soon rise and then to the horse which pawed the ground and then back at her as if to say, time is wasting and hurry with yourself and we need to get down the road.

When he turned his look a second time in her direction she was pulling the trousers onto her hips and cinching them with the belt. She was telling him she would from now on not be Rachel to him but a boy just like he was and if it came down to it she was his brother. She would be Ray. It's what her mother used to call her. At least it's what she remembered. Then the shirt and the jacket. With the prospect of escape and her decision made, she now could not move fast enough. She could not stop talking. She insisted that he understand how important this was and he told her he did. He told her he understood.

She sat on the ground and dragged the socks and then the shoes onto her feet and it was when she was tying the laces there was a rustling inside the cow barn and a groan and the man came stumbling out. He was so desperate to relieve himself he did not see them until he'd unbuttoned himself and his piss was steaming on the ground.

"Pay no attention to me," he said, as if he found the moment amusing.

He then finished his business and buttoned up after wagging himself dry. He approached the girl and when he reached to touch her clipped head she swatted at his hand and backed away from him.

"What happened to your goldilocks?" he said, pretending a posture of meticulousness and refinement, his hand still raised. "You know you don't sell for what you're worth unless you look good."

Rachel seemed paralyzed by him, her words stolen from her mind, her determination vanished. He felt it himself, the honeyed voice and created gestures. The man's size ran to proportion that was beyond his physical being. He asserted himself into the world, as if he should possess other human beings and they should willingly submit to him. Somewhere a cock began to crow and the light changed as if a first curtain had been drawn open on the day to come.

"We have to go," Robey said. He'd already drawn the Remington from his belt and the angle at which he held it, though not pointing at the man, declared his intention to use it.

"Who the hell are you?"

"None of your damn business," he said. He wanted to tell the man who he was and what he'd seen and what he'd endured and what he'd lost, but he had no reason to be known by him, to be known by anyone.

"But you are going?" the man said to the girl, his voice demonstrating how incredible he thought the idea.

"We're going," Robey told him.

"I will come for her," he said. "You know that."

"It's a big country."

"It ain't that big."

"No, I 'spect it ain't."

"Then take the horse," the man said to her as if he were that generous.

"I don't want your god damn horse," the girl spat out.

"That isn't Christian," the man said.

"You shut up your god damn mouth, you old blister." She held her hands over her ears. She hated him. She did not want to hear what he had to say. "You sinned against my flesh," she cried.

"Rachel," he said, her name in a voice sweet as the vine.

"He wears a money belt of stol'd money," she said, her eyes

closed and her hands still clapped to the sides of her head. "Get it."

"Where is it?" Robey said.

"Don't be a dunce," she told him. "It's around his waist."

"I will find you," the man said. "You know I will find you."

"Shut your hole," she said, and this turned him mean as he understood his hold on her was breaking.

"You will rue this day as long as you live," he told her. "When I find you, you will regret you ever treated me this way."

"You did this to me," she said, "and what did I do to deserve this. You are the one who'll pay in hell."

The man suddenly went down on his knees in a stylish and practiced gesture. He closed his eyes and clasped his hands to his breast as if in prayer and his pursed lips began to pulse as if his silent prayer was so profound it required release. She paused in her anger for how dramatic an effect this had on her.

"Please forgive me," he said to her, and then he let his prayers be aloud and they came in a torrent, rote and passionately, about the sins of men and the frailties of human flesh.

She told him to stop, to please stop and then to stop his jabbering, but his fervor increased as he struggled to reach dominion over her mind.

"Don't do that," she cried, and kicked at him. "God damn you," she screamed. "I hate you."

Robey stood witness to them in their opposite struggles, the crying girl who sought escape and the cruel praying man who had harmed her. He knew the scene had been played before in tents and sheds and under the bowers of trees. He could see the past, the power and belligerence of the man's imprecations. He could see them wearing down the girl and turning her against herself and making her forget her own experience at his very hands and hostile to her own wishes.

She stamped the ground and cried that he should shut his praying mouth and should kill himself to death for all he'd done in life. His words continued on, penetrating the air with their ferocity, and were so like falling wood and she screamed at him to stop, but he wouldn't stop. A moan came from deep inside the barn. The woman had awakened in darkness and was calling out for someone to help her.

"Make him stop," she told Robey. "Put him through," she said, and grabbed for the Remington he held, but he would not let her have it. He'd stood by and watched this man harm her and he had done nothing when he could have. It was not so much that he felt guilt for not acting that night in the fire-gutted house. He was different then and now he was changed. Then he was a boy, and he thought like a boy. He angered and hated, but he thought the world still had a chance. He thought they all had a chance. Perhaps somewhere inside him he knew his fate and that night in the fire-gutted house it was not time yet for him to leave his past and enter his future, but only the damned can see their future and know nothing of their present.

No matter. He had already made his decision. What was another man like this man to him? The praying man wanted her forgiveness. It may have been true. But sometimes you have to revenge before you can forgive. Familiar to his ears was how loud and certain the mechanical sound at his thigh when he thumbed the hammer on the Remington. If the praying man heard the same sound, his voice did not betray him.

He raised his hand to sight the barrel with the praying man's forehead and was to pull the trigger when the girl dashed in between them. With both her hands, she raised a long-handled implement above her right shoulder. At its highest reach she did not stop but drove it down with all her might and as hard as she could, and in that instant the three thin tines of a pitchfork pierced into the praying man's kneeling lap.

They were like fangs the way they entered into him. They were a sharp curving blink that found no bone in their sharp passage. They stopped his praying and opened his eyes with burning pain. His lap was suddenly on fire. She jumped her weight at the handle and drove it again and it was this second effort that overcame the silence of shock and delivered to the heavens the screams of the well stabbed.

He let down the hammer of the Remington, belted it, and pulled her away by her shaking shoulders. She fought him because she wanted to jump the fork a third time and send it deeper, even though deeper was not a possibility.

So much killing and so much violence. So much malice and fraud. He saw them. He saw her. He saw the praying man and he saw himself. How to explain the way violence needs violence? Is that the explanation itself? Violence demands violence. This was not the pagan retribution: an eye for an eye, a tooth for a tooth. This was the law before there was law. This was vengeance and a rebellion to law. How to explain the failure to understand this and the failure to not understand there are things that cannot be understood?

He knew in the end there were no answers. There was no illumination. The world was chance and was not revealed to us, but it revealed us to ourselves, our fragments of idea, our false memory. There was neither vision nor wisdom to be discovered. We only became more seeing and less ignorant. Sin could not be washed away and minds do not heal except for the guilty and the foolish. Our confessions become our weakness and our wisdom our vanity and both our harmful fantasies. He looked at the praying man and knew one thing: we have chosen ourselves to be the chosen.

He thought his father's words and then he thought about the girl as she struggled in his arms to reach the handle and drive it again. He feared she would not return from where she had just been. He had thought that maybe she had a different way of looking at the world whereas he had none that he knew of anymore and just maybe she was a way back for him, but now he did not know. He only knew he could not let her kill the man any more than she already had. As he held her, he held the moment of life in his hands, his own life.

He looked to the praying man and he appeared to still be doing so. His hands were raised in supplication and his mouth gaped and tears streamed down his straining face. He fought movement for how consuming the pain that had discovered him, but his body could not endure the pain and wanted to reject its source and so the handle of the pitchfork quivered in the air as his body tried to tremble it out.

Robey pulled the girl away from the man to the side of the coal black horse. He took her foot and placed it in the stirrup and then with both hands he heaved her into the saddle. He began to walk and the coal black horse followed him.

THEY TRAVELED SOUTH on the coal black horse, leaving that place of the dead. He could feel her body slumped against his back, her arms clasped around his waist. When they were chased, she rapped on his head with her knuckles and he turned an ear to her speaking lips. She told him to ride into the fog, but the horse already knew to do so and was already disappearing inside a vast gray cloud come to earth.

On that ride to the river, all time was present time. There was no past and there was no future. They were beginning in their flight and rode the coal black horse hard like a fleeing deer. They might this time leave the earth, he thought. They might ride through the sky. They might ride forever until it was all behind them, until it was over.

What he remembered was the silence of that leaving and it was a very complete silence. He sensed that those men who offered blood and presented blood and threw blood were not ravaged by war, but for all the dirt and black powder and slick of blood they had been prepared by war, prepared for their irrevocable and irreversible deaths. The wounds were horrible enough, but only of a kind. They had their faces or did not by increasing degree until there were men with no faces at all and in the end it was remarkable to him how little there was that can be done to a man once all that can be done has been done to him.

He had experienced the horror that leaves you calm and unafraid, but for her something inside was broken and he did not know if it could be be mended. Her life, her horror, he could not tell.

As they rode out of there and down that road, the pink and green dawn came and the sun when it rose looked to be a globe of red-hot iron. The air was still and heated, and as if that were not enough, women and children could be seen piling wood on dead horses and setting them afire. Their immense bodies lay on the ground, their elegant necks and finely shaped heads, the round spring of ribs. For miles were the collapsed and bulge-eyed beasts and in places the ground was blackened with their grease where someone had already burned one of them. He remembered also the sight of those two ladies sitting in their open doorway selling water and laughing as if nothing had happened and he thought what a strange world it had become and he could not understand it enough even to tell of it if someone had asked him.

It was days afterward and miles south when the rain-washed air began to clear of its death smell and they were at the banks of the Potomac where they stole their way into the lines. On their heels, as if in pursuit of their own persons, the Federal Army had finally mustered and appeared in the fields and woods beyond the sentries.

By then the field works were up and the engineers were completing a pontoon bridge to make the crossing. They were as if an ancient forlorn people gathered on the grim shore of an old river. He found Moxley and Yandell and Tom Allen. They were with the battery as his father had said they would be. He told them he was Robey Childs and they told how his father was good as gold and if anybody ever needed him he always came a-runnin'. He was the bravest man any of them ever knew.

Thereafter, they would call him captain, as they had called his father, and that night he sent off a letter to his mother but could not bear to tell her all he knew.

As to Rachel, the men of the battery said nothing to him. It was a mystery to them what was between the son of their fallen comrade and this girl who traveled with him posing as a boy, but they made no judgment and spoke not a word of it among themselves.

After Gettysburg the rain had resumed with a vengeance. Rolling thunder shook the night's darkness. The rains were torrential and the lightning flashes left them momentarily blind. They sat in the rain with the water running from the cuffs of their jackets, waiting for the crossing.

Finally came the nights of July 13 and 14, wet and black, and these were the nights they chose to escape across the pontoon bridge. Supplies were critically short. Men were hungry and picking kernels of corn out of the horse dung. With tarpaulins they sheltered their smoky fires of green and snapping pine logs, so they would continue burning and give the impression that men still fed them. All that day a line of the tallest men, their arms locked together, had stretched from bank to bank so others might make the crossing. Then the word went around that the river was falling steadily and that the thin line of the pontoon bridge had been completed.

On a rainy and foggy night torches were lit and bonfires were built of fence rails to light the way to the other side. Robey and Rachel waited in the gravel at the dissolving edge of the river as the water rose and curled. When it descended, they rode the coal black horse onto the bridge, cut loose its mooring and under a wetting drizzle, the blossoms dropping in the water, they floated to Virginia.

16

PERIOD OF SHADOW drapes from her shoulder to the swell of her small belly as if a length of long black hair. In a flawless china sky the sun is bright and coming through the panes of glass as it makes its crossing east to west.

He is asleep, sitting up in a chair beside her. His hands are palms down on his knee caps. A loaded Springfield rifle lays on the floor at his feet and beside it the six-shot Remington. She thinks she's had a dream and she's frightened. She cannot separate what she dreams from what she thinks.

They travel nights and sleep by day and it will soon be dark again and time to travel the twisting roads one day closer to home. Getting himself home. At night the darkening air brings silence before the walk of the predators, the hunters. For them the night will bring invisible passage for their escape.

"Would you like to live here?" she said, turning her head slowly.

"No," he said, as a sleep-talker without waking. "I wouldn't want to live here."

"Where would you want to live?"

"Where I am from."

"There's too much light out," she said. "Can't we sleep at night?"

He'd already told her so many times before that they couldn't sleep at night. They slept by day and at night they traveled to travel unseen. She pulled the blanket to her shoulders and moved her arms beneath its drape, and when she did she was strangely limbless and birdlike, her arms winged and flightless in the windless, airless room.

"It ain't safe," he said, and stretched out his legs, a boot heel banging on the floor. It was getting late in the day, and now awake he'd not be able to sleep again before it was time to leave.

"I dreamt we were asleep together," she said.

Her voice was matter-of-fact and he thought she meant him, in her dream, together with her. But he did not presume she meant him and so wondered whose dream company she was recounting. She carried her life with her and could not flee from it, even in her sleep. She tossed and turned and cried out in her sleep. She insisted upon sleeping with her knife and that he keep the blade sharp. It was inside her and knocking at her ribs and fluttering her lungs as if they were wings startled and throbbing with urgency.

"You should try to sleep a little," he said. He'd told her this so many times before and was beginning to understand that opposite his intentions, he was counseling her in the direction of her terror.

"Where do you think she disappeared to?"

"I don't know," he said, sitting up and looking about the room as if there were still the presence of a third person.

In the house where they lodged was a raggedy old woman with a sun-stained and stroke-twisted face. One of her eyes was bloodshot and the other was as white and round as an ivory marble. She had welcomed them into her house and with a hand grinder she had made flour and with the flour she had made balls of dough as big as her gnarled fist. She fried potatoes for them to eat, and there was bacon, and she made up a sack of the same for them to take when they rode away. She had moved about the house as if a phantom impaired and more than once burned herself as she cooked and took an awfully long time to realize it. As her presence in the house seemed odd to herself, they inquired but could not sort from her if it was her house or not.

What they did learn was that her ears did not work too good and so it was hard for her to hear them from both sides of her head at once. They learned she had not seen a soul for months, not even a stray dog, and they learned she had a son named Horace. He was a crackerjack of a young man, but he had been killed by which side she did not know and what did it matter anyhow? She declared her heart and mind were broken by it. She knew this, she said, but she claimed love and prayer were enough to get by on. She declared herself a good saint of God regardless of what he had done to her. When she said these things there was a breath around her that shined as if it was not air or light but was something from within.

"I can't sleep without knowing where she's at," Rachel said. "Do you think she's still wandering about? She gives me the cold shivers."

"Try counting," he said. He rubbed his face hard, as if trying to rearrange his features. He wanted to comfort her, but she contained inside a wall of vigilance and suspicion she had built around herself. Not since she had comforted him upon the death of his father had she acted kindly toward him.

"One, two, three," she said. "It doesn't work."

That was when he told her he loved her.

"Why?" she said.

"I just do."

She raised her draped arms and slowly turned her face to him. The point of her knife prodded the blanket material.

"Don't be such a straw-head," she scoffed.

She lay back down on the divan in the strange room, pulled the blanket to her chin. She turned to face the back of the divan and pretended sleep. She was exhausted for the weight she carried inside her and did not understand why she shouldn't be able to sleep, why he should say he loved her.

"I almost love you," she said, relenting, and was to say more but was stricken by her own words and shook her head violently—no, she did not mean to say what she said. She seemed ashamed of her mistrust, or inability, he did not know which. As time had gone by his mind had increasingly become confused when it came to her. He wondered if the debt he was paying could ever be paid, or if she even thought about it that way, or knew how he thought about it.

"How much longer?" she said.

"A few more days," he said softly. "Rest a while and we will go."

Their stay with the battery on the banks of the Potomac had been brief. He secured a hard-mouthed bay mare for her to ride, the rare horse that the coal black horse would tolerate, as well as provisions, ammunition, a brass telescope, and the Springfield. The army was still precariously encamped when he asked the men of the battery how far it would be home and how long it would take. They told him two days if he didn't sleep and killed the horse in getting there. Otherwise it would take five days. He was to figure 150 mile as the crow flies and ride by night and each day rub down the horses.

Hole up by day and sleep with the sun, they told him, and when there's nothing left and there's five miles to go, cut deep gashes in the horses' shoulders and pour gun powder into their open wounds. Yessir, by the Jesus, that's what they would do to get home in a hurry. But then again, riding that black horse to death ain't worth gettin' to anybody's home and who the fuck needs a home when you got a horse as fine as that one?

They'd ridden hard the past days and in their imaginations it was as if the whole world was chasing them. They slept under rock ledges and in hollow logs and moved their position when he had the instinct to do so and each dawn they halted again. The highways were beset with a confusion of regular and irregular troops. There were partisans and bushwhackers. There were profits to be taken and old scores to settle. He'd learned in no uncertain way that this was war too, name it the war inside war. No matter, it was as much a part of war as war itself and in war you get killed just for living.

Their shortest route was west by southwest but this took them against the intentions of all flowing water and the corrugated upthrust of every folded mountain. They crossed rivers and streams and waded dense sloughs and after a time he could glimpse the green front of the Alleghenies they would have to ascend. In places the front was ramped foothills and stone-bound windy gaps and in other places flat walls of forested stone and cobbly switchbacks and the whole effect was like that of a great resting beast, its legs tucked beneath its body and its paws extended from beneath its chest.

"Two, three more days," he said.

"Nights, you mean."

"Nights," he agreed.

He worried her mind would give out in that time. It had become that bitter and was that near to its breaking point. It seemed she had not slept as long as he had known her. She held to her fear and her mind would not give it up no matter how hard she tried to persuade it into a different direction. She began to tremble and then she sat up and let the blanket and then the dirty sleep shirt slide off her shoulders.

"Lay on top of me," she said, letting the knife slip to the floor from her hand and laying back and opening her arms to reveal her naked body. But he did not move. He was not sure he could move.

She called to him again and told him what to do and when he still did not move she told him if he wanted to marry her he had better be nice to her.

He was clumsy in his movement. He moved to sit beside her on the divan and then let himself forward to be caught by her and in a tangle of arms and blanket and sleep shirt he was pulled down against her body.

"Don't move," she said, and held him to her shaking body.

He let his face to her skin and breathed in the smell of leather and sweat and horse and wood smoke they both shared. He wanted his face against her skin and to not move it. He could feel something pulled from inside him and extending toward her. He wanted to say words that would tell her this, but his feelings were not clear to him and they would not be for a long time.

"You aren't the worst," she said with sweet resignation, and pulled him even closer to her body than he already was. She stroked his back and kissed his cheek and neck.

When they awoke the old woman was still absent the house and at first they did not talk about her and the longer they waited for the other to mention her absence, the more impossible it became to acknowledge she had even existed. He stepped out into the yard and scanned the circle of the horizon. He cradled the Springfield in the crook of his elbow. It would be dark soon. Sun-fires lit the western horizon as the sun in its setting was burning down the earth.

He wandered the yard and there was still no sign of the old woman. Then the curl of a low branch at the edge of the porch caught his eye through the porch railing. At first he thought it the tiny face of a child peeking at him from the bushes or the tiny face of a shy wood sprite caught in mischief. He stepped onto the porch and cocked his head and saw what it was: a whorl of dried needles that looked nothing like the face of a tiny child or wood sprite. He tilted his head again and his eye could barely catch what he'd seen, but there it was again.

"I see you," he said.

He played this game until his mind could find face and then left off to bridle and saddle the horses. When he went back inside Rachel was at the sugar chest, wetting her finger in her mouth and feeding sweet scrapings onto her tongue. He watched her eat the sugar and when she looked up he encouraged her to continue until she'd had her fill.

"Have your dinner," she said, and led him to the stove for potatoes and bacon. He was hungry and, no utensils at hand, he took up the plate and ate the heated food with his fingers.

They mounted the horses in darkness and rode into the ink black night and when they stopped to rest the horses she told him she was in a better state of mind but still far from feeling the way she wanted to.

"I thought it would get better by now," she said, "but it hasn't."

He made to speak, but the words would not come. He wanted to tell her it was a matter of time, but did he know this to be true? He carried his own sadness and hatred and to these his mind was fastened and enlivened. He did not want to forget, not ever. How could he suggest she move on from her own? He led with his hands, as if words were found by touch until finally he gave up and let his hands drop into his lap.

She waited to see if that was all he had to say and then she laughed at him.

He found for her a can of condensed milk, punched it with the point of her knife and this they shared beneath a grotto of stone where a spring ran out while the watered horses cooled in a stand of trees. His eyes searched the shadowy patterns of the starlit forest. He was calculating another move tonight, weighing the advantage of another mile against what it might cost to her and the animals. He knew the bay would soon give out, but they were close now. He did not know this ground, but he knew the terrain and recognized how it would lead them through.

"The stars have moved closer," he said, squatting beside her. He made up his mind; they would spend the duration of that night where they were and make one more move before daybreak.

"Do you think she was ever there?" she asked of the old woman where they had spent the day.

"I don't know," he said. "I never thought she wasn't."

"It's probably just as well," she said.

As to staying where they were, he suddenly changed his

mind and they climbed into their saddles once again. He needed to get home. He needed to return to his mother to know she was safe.

EARLY IN THE MORNING they saw turkey vultures sailing the uplifts, the air above the air, and their eccentric rises and descents were slow and screwlike. Old wood smoke still filtered through the pines, a stove fire let slowly to die. There was an old woman wearing a shawl and carrying an umbrella. Beside her was an old man leaning on a walking stick. They were watching the sunrise from a hilltop and then they moved on and disappeared behind the hill. He took them to be more of the nice women and good men staggered and shattered by the spiral of events begun and that once begun begat their own private, terrible, and willful force.

When they reached the place, it had the look of abandonment after years of decline. For some reason he had the instant passing memory of a complete story his father told him about an ancient athlete who ran up a mountain with a newborn bull calf on his shoulders. He did this every day in the belief that as the bull calf grew he would likewise build himself and become a stronger man. His father declared it to be an impossibility but an idea capable of dogging the mind. Maybe bull calves didn't grow so fast in ancient times as they did now. No matter. His father said that he could never give up the thought of that man and despite what he knew to be true about growing bulls, he sometimes still wondered why it couldn't work.

Aside from the obvious reasons, why not? his father had opinioned. It's the kind of idea that holds sway on the thinking mind. Maybe all people were this same way. Maybe they carried on in belief against a bad idea but nevertheless carried on until it collapsed them.

The cabin door bore a huge iron padlock, sized for an armory or a ship, and the cabin seemed to wear it not for its security but as if in punishment for grave transgression. Likewise, the shutters were nailed fast, but contrarily the kitchen garden had been recently tended and what used to be flower beds of considerable proportions still bloomed with garish heads tottering above new weeds. Wild roses chafed at the log walls. There was a cistern filled by a wooden pipe with amber-colored water. There was a neatness that made him think the old people would be returning in a day or so.

He called out, and as he expected he received no reply. The only sound to be heard was that of the horses tearing and champing sweet clover and the trickling of the water's ropey fall from the pipe's end.

The sty they found empty and overgrown with thistle and the sty's earth was dry and settled. There'd been no rooting hog that season and runner vines had curled and woven the barked and gnawed logs. Orange trumpetlike flowers toppled on their green stems. They moved on to the stable searching for inhabitants. Inside its board walls it smelled of mildew and clay, the ferment of manure and hay. In one stall was the rotting smell of seed potatoes gone unplanted.

Out the back door on a grassy sward they discovered the attraction of the gyring vultures. In the trampled grass was a maiden mare and a new foal lying beside each other as if died in parturition. The mare had thrown down the foal bed and her shrunken pear-shaped womb lay to her hocks, blackening in the switch grass and pea-vine. The feet of the newborn foal were frayed and flaky and still wore a fringe of soft horn so young he speculated it was preborn.

"She were a very fine horse," he said of the mare.

"Do you think they've gone somewheres?" she said, her throat constricted with the grisly spectacle they witnessed but did not want to acknowledge.

"Recent," he said, and told her how he'd seen them through the telescope departing on their approach. He speculated the death of a mare such as her was enough to break a frail spirit.

The sun was most risen when they washed in the cistern and fried bacon and onions they took from the garden. There were also baby carrots and tomatoes. After they ate she undressed and rinsed her clothes in the cistern and then she decided to climb in after them and wash herself. There was no suggestion that he look or not look and in her immersion she found peaceful occupation. She let the trickling water run through her hair and splashed him and told him that he ought to take a bath because he stank to high heaven. He kicked off his boots and still wearing his clothes climbed in too. She thought this funny and laughed and then coaxed them from him and as he gave her each article she scrubbed and beat and wrung the water from them. His hands and neck and face were burned nut brown from the wind and sun. She inspected his head wound and declared it to be nicely scarred.

They draped their clothes over low bushes in the sunlight and wrapped themselves in blankets. She wanted to sleep in the grass under the shade of a tree, but he insisted they sleep in the stable with the horses. So, exhausted, they closed the stable door and bedded down to sleep the day. The darkness inside was incomplete but crosshatched with thin shafts of infiltrating sunlight.

He told her the light stems traveled in the straightest lines to be found in the natural world.

She held her hand up and slowly moved it until it found one. She then pulled away as if burned or cut and laughed at how funny the game she was playing. She returned her hand and let the light play on her open palm and then touched her palm to her face as if to carry its warmth to her skin.

At her insistence they lay close together to whisper, even to touch. He felt her breath dance on his face as light as an eyelash. He felt the air in the barn cool on his skin. His eyes found her eyes and she looked away.

"He ain't dead," she said.

"No, he probably ain't."

"He'll come, you know. Sure as heaven and earth. She's dying and he'll come for me."

She continued to play in the light as her thoughts let words to her mouth. She let herself look into his eyes and then she pretended to carry the warmth to his face, his cheeks, his eyes, his forehead, the lines in her hand pressed and held against his skin.

"He ain't like anybody I ever met," he said, "and I have met some odd ones."

"You can't listen to him talk or he'll change you," she whispered as if it was a mortal secret. "He is the mesmerizer. He opens his mouth and begins to preach and they're walking the aisles, ya-hooing and boo-hooing." She deepened her voice and mock intoned, "How does a black cow eat green grass and produce white milk, yellow butter, and orange cheese? Don't you tell me there isn't a God. Ya-hoo. Boo-hoo."

He asked her who she was to the man and the woman and how they came to be traveling together.

She told him her father was a preacher in Baltimore and had answered a call to mission in Africa for two years. She told him her father was a true man of God who always said there's a thick black line between okay and the right way. It was when her mother and father left for Africa the man and the woman were assigned to be her guardians until their return. But her mother and father were killed in that far-off country.

"Their riverboat overturned and they swam ashore and were attacked by a lion."

"A lion?" he said, as if their existence were confirmed.

"A lion."

"God, I never knew anyone kilt by a lion."

"It's not an everyday thing," she said.

She continued to talk as if once begun she could not stop. She told him one day he'd scream at her and the next day he'd beg forgiveness. He commanded her life and no decisions were her own.

"I was going to run off," she said, "but I guess I just run off too late for my own good."

"A person can get used to just about anything if it happens slow enough," he said.

"Not that," she spat, and then she turned her back and went silent on him and they did not speak again before sleep.

Late that day when he broke from sleep it was because he could not breathe. He thought to feel hands on his chest and at his throat, so difficult it was for him to receive air. He turned over and on all fours he hacked and coughed. His eyes stung and his face was as if poisoned. The stable was filled with smoke, the horses stamping and screaming, their hooves knocking on their wooden stalls. At first he could make nothing of this noise and smoke. His mind moved slowly and then all at once. The stable was on fire.

Half suffocated, he crawled naked for the door, but it would not open. The flames were close and had begun to roar for the heat they generated. He kicked at the door with both his feet and it gave with each blow but fell back and he could not hold it enough to squeeze through. It was chained or jammed, he did not know which. He pawed at the earth beneath it and then finding a broken shovel he dug with that and flattening his body he was able to scrape underneath. Outside, he waited to be shot, but the shot never came. He held to the earth and breathed deeply and from where he lay he could see gray smoke pouring from the windows and snaking across the roof. Above the door the track had separated and a wheel was stuck in the gap.

He cut away his hold on the earth and lifted and tore at the door with all of his strength until the door, track and all, fell away from the opening and a wall of black smoke poured from the opening. He crawled back inside, breathing the lean air close to the ground and found her lost and struggling and fought with her and dragged her free as the coal black horse found the opening and bolted through with the bay mare following behind.

From that moment on her panic returned and would not abate. Her hands shook and her thoughts came from her in a frenzy or not all, but mostly not at all. He thought how barn doors, worn with constant use, were always coming off their tracks and it could have been just that, but he did not know

how the flames could have started or why. He searched his
memory as to when they ate and where they built their cook
fire and whether or not he sufficiently doused it. And if it was
someone who'd lit that fire, why did they not shoot him when
he crawled to the air? He could not answer these questions,
and as night fell on that day he concluded he never would.

In those next hours they experienced the sense of being
pushed before consequence while carrying it with them.
Their bodies were in the fugue state of turmoil and relentless fatigue that is felt by both the hunter and the hunted.
They rode out of there, abreast and in step, the horses' hooves
powdering the red-soil dust of the valley floor. He carried the
Springfield floating upright, the butt resting on his thigh, as
they dodged through the dense forests enameled green in the
unfriendly daylight and the horses played and lathering, they
continued on, traveling into the night, all the while looking
back and waiting for the gunshots that never came.

He insisted they travel the long way by woodland lanes and
pathless crosscuts and from time to time they took refuge
in cool starlit woods where they hoped they would be safe.
When he heard hoof beats, they bushed up and waited in
blackness and soon he could hear the ring of so many pounding hooves it was as if an entire calvary was pursuing them.
He understood there was no reason for them to be pursued,
but he wanted no encounter, no delay, no possibility of all the
trouble there was to be found on the roads in those days after
Gettysburg. They waited and watched and the sound grew
and then it bore off and there were no sounds and the night
returned to silence.

He pointed to her the stars that guided him in case she

needed them. In the northwest was Ursa Major, the bear, and in the northeast of that month the first stars of the Great Square of Pegasus were rising above the horizon. There is Polaris, he told her, the North Star.

"If anything ever happens," he said, "don't you worry about me. Just start running."

She assured him he had nothing to worry about on that account.

They waited until they were sure the road was clear and then crossed over and struck through the open countryside and by then it was close to morning. They found a path, a ribbon that went winding between the willow stems and it was there they lost the bay. She came up lame in her right foreleg, so tender she would not let down her leg. A hairline crack in the hoof wall had split open and the frog was likewise split and hot and raw.

He hiked Rachel into the saddle of the coal black horse and led them for a while and then he mounted behind her and they rode double under the waning moon, a half shell in the sky, west through the measureless dark forest.

17

HERE THE MERCANTILE had once stood was burned over and now a blackened patch of ground. The fire had spread and consumed the lean-to stable where first he had seen the coal black horse. It had climbed to the rock walls that stood behind the stable and now the rocks were scorched black and leaked variegated runnels of coppery water. The smith was likewise burned to the ground and where it had stood was now a junkyard of iron and charred timbers. In the center stood the great anvil, untoppled and settled upright, as if it rode the burning stump upon which it rested down to the ground to wait patiently for the next hammer that would presume to strike it.

There was no sign of old Morphew or the hunchback German or the upside-down boy. There was no sign that human life had been recent and one day would resume. The site was lonesome and haunting and its borders already greening and closing over with the nature that would repossess it.

They did not linger in that place but rode on into the hollow in precise reverse of the descent he had made what seemed so long ago. He was now different. He was older and born over and had lived out the ends of so many men's lives, his father's life.

In this dry season the leaned-out Canaan was pools and riffles fed by tiny veins of feeder streams. The Twelve Mile was the same, but its water was colder and blacker and its banks more grown and wild with the tough and sunless varieties. Trees had toppled into the moaty water and raised to the air great fans of scrabbled roots that clutched boulders in their twisted fingers. Sweeping trunks of mountain laurel met, intersected, and wove together and all about was as if a ferocious and violent nature had walled the mountain in waiting for his return.

They rode on, higher and higher, and found a sunken place near the bridge that once spanned its surface where stone and gravel had washed in. The coal black horse, without hesitation, stepped off from the bank and forded the slow cooling flow, belly deep and sure-footed.

The air closed and cooled around them as they continued their ascent and late that day they came upon the old fields grown with mullein and yarrow and then was the high meadow in the sling of the mountain wreathed in juniper, and it was a flash of wet grass in a startle of sunlight when they broke from the rock walls and stepped out on what seemed the top of the world.

The cabin, when he finally saw it, was smaller than he remembered and in the time since his departure seemed to have endured a great weather. Its logs were cracked and silvered and its cedar roofing was lifted, twisted, and ramshackled by the torment of a vagrant wind. Slivers quilled the rounds, and moss and vine were abundant in their reclamation. No aspect was square. No surface had yet to begin its return to nature and yet all seemed perched and more precarious than a balanced eye.

But there was a greenness and an abundance he'd not imagined possible. It was as if the garden, the fields, and the mountain had blossomed. There were new lambs gamboling on the hillside and stiff-legged spring calves blatting for their mothers. A litter of mewling pups gadded about. It was as if his mother had bred animals and increased nature to replace men and children. It was as if he had returned to the realm of dreams.

He dismounted and crossed the cabin's threshold. She could see him in her mirror when he stepped through the doorway. She was touching her wild hair as if anticipating an arrival, as if it were an aspect of her being newly recognized.

"Who's there?" she said fondly, because she already knew it was him. "Come out of the shadows where I can see you," she said, and it was only then the dogs flattened their ears and rose up bristling for how fooled they were by his approach. They exploded with deep shocked barks, slobbering and clacking jaws and the scratching of the paws skittering on the rough floor to reach their lumbrous bodies between her and him. They could not hide their embarrassment when they saw who it was.

"They've known you were coming," she said in their defense. "They just didn't know when. They have been antsy for days."

Her hair had whitened and her face had taken on the purity that is found in the sick and the holy and the season-changing sky. She moved about with steps so silent she was as if nature in transit drifting the floorboards. She'd not seen another human being since he left. She'd not heard another human voice and had long since left her own voice inside her head as the faintest whisper of sound enough for the animals to hear when they were called to milk or feed or from one pasture to the next.

"You've been gone a very long time," she said. "Are you really here?" She touched his face in the manner of the reading sightless.

"Did you receive my letter," he said.

"No," she said. "It hasn't come yet, but it will."

It was then she let go the slender hope that her husband, her son's father, was still alive. She knew then he would not come stamping across the threshold and take her in his arms and lift her off her feet.

But she had long since entered the world of loss and enduring silence and now was the beginning of its infinite and companionable grief. Later she would tell him she'd dreamed his father was dead and admitted she was not shocked when he did not arrive home. She just didn't know until then it was actually true. But she'd never dreamed Robey dead and so looked for him every day and thought he would surely come home to her.

"You must be tired," she said looking past her son to the girl.

"I need to lay down," she said. "I am so tired and my shoulders ache."

His mother directed her to sit by the window in the cushioned chair and then he followed her into the kitchen where, composed and inhabiting herself again, she daubed grease into a skillet.

"Who is she?" she finally said as the grease popped and she let the eggs slide in to fry. "Where does she come from?"

"I don't know much about her," he said.

When she turned and looked at him, she could see that he had changed. She could not imagine what he had seen while he was gone. She could not imagine the black curve he carried inside him. But no, he hadn't changed. He was her son and the change was from a boy to a man and that was to be expected.

"What did she tell you?"

"We talked some."

"What did you talk about?"

"I wonder about that sometimes."

"I'd like your part of the story," his mother coaxed, but this conversation was not her interest. It was simply an effort to fill the silence.

"She said her mother and father was killed in Africa."

"That seems an awful place to die."

"There are better ones?" he asked.

"I think I'd prefer my own bed for one, but then I am not the world traveler you have become."

His face flushed red with shame and he wanted to apologize, but he said nothing. He sat with her while she cooked eggs and bacon and there was bread in the warming oven. She gave account of the farm, its progress, and the necessary work to be done now that he had returned.

THAT NIGHT ON THE MOUNTAIN while the women slept, he sat outside in the cool summer air, the coal black horse staked to a long lead. In the farthest distance he could see the faint glimmer of a light and then another one. They were miles away and lights he'd never seen before. When his mother came out she was wearing her nightgown and a sweater and carrying for him another plate of food. He apologized to her for being a smart mouth and wished to take it back and she accepted his apology and agreed to let him.

"That's a fine horse you've brought home," she said.

"I owe Mister Morphew for it," he told her, and explained how he'd lent it to him, but he did not yet tell her the mercantile was burned out and so too the smith. Instead he asked after the distant lights and she told him they'd been burning for a month.

"They must be homesteaders," she said. "There were bonfires at first."

"Homesteaders," he said. The thought was incredible to him. Did they not know what was going on in the world?

He then said in answer to the question he knew she was thinking, "It's a hard place to talk about what happened east."

"There's time," she said, and then with a sigh that escaped her, "Time's what we have now."

"He told me to tell you he loved you more than anything on earth."

When he said these words to her they broke her and she tried hard not to, but she began to weep. He thought of all the tearful women, the mothers and daughters and lovers weeping for the men and boys who were lost souls no longer in possession of living bodies. They were prisoners of their dreams to come and powerless over their dominion. He thought of the men and boys who would come home and would never heal, the broken and wounded, the not dead. Those who would never see, never walk, never chew food, never speak a word, never sit up, never dress themselves, never again have a thought in their minds. What would their women do? Would they still love the men and boys? What would love become? He thought better dead and lost than maimed and crippled.

She cried until her shoulders caved and she could not breathe. She choked, but when he tried to hold her she would not let him. He knew she wanted to be alone but understood that she did not want to do it by herself. He sat quietly with his hands folded and ready.

Then it passed and she gathered herself and wiped at her face with the backs of her hands. There was a long silence until she spoke again.

"Do you know she is going to have a baby?"

"No," he said, shaking his head. "I didn't know that."

"Is it yours?"

"If she wants it to be."

That night they sat under the stars long past tiredness as they did not want to be separate from each other's company after so long apart. They watched the distant lights flickering against the atmosphere that existed between them and the homesteaders.

He wondered aloud if it was wind or mist or maybe some-one had crossed in front of a window between them and the light that made it come and go. He wondered to himself how she must have known Rachel was going to have a baby and thought back to those days on the road and when he did his mind failed him. Could she have burned the stable? She was already a mystery to him and so the news of her having a baby made little difference to his mind. If she had tried to burn, what difference did it make now?

Together they listened to the intermittent call of the night birds and the sawing sound that is made by grazing animals. For neither of them was the reunion complete and joyful, but they would gratefully receive what was left to them as they watched together the moon set beneath their feet, beyond the rim of the earth.

THEY WERE NOW in the cooling weather of the fall and descending in the country was haunting autumnal stillness. The sky was high and smoky-colored and mornings the fodder was frosted with hoary crystals and steamed in the air when broke open. The sun came flat and its light was not warm but white and cold. From miles away plied the wet smoke of burned slash as somewhere in the country more land was being cleared with fire. However pleasant that summer had been, however abundant the crops and productive the stock, it was the harbinger of the darker days to come.

It was not strange to him how his mother had grieved that summer as she experienced, drop by drop, the pain of pain remembered. Early morning, midday, and after supper she would disappear from their table, lost and broken-hearted, and into the fields, into the forest, into darkness, and he would hear her stirring in the night preparing to go and he would follow her into the night always at a distance and always she would be comforted by his watchful presence. He would cut the pain from her if he could. It was as if when she ate she fed grief into her mouth and when she walked she took it into her legs and when she carried, she bore it in her arms and shoulders and slowly and imperceptibly she was altered.

It was during that summer Rachel's belly began to grow and as it did her body diminished as if consumed and contained within her prodigious belly would be an astonishing yield and when delivered there would be nothing left of her and she would disappear. His mother engaged her with activity, prodded her when she moped, and by dint of will refused her the deep blueness she would surely have sunk into. He did not know what was between them. He knew it was not a peaceful understanding but was an understanding distant and by appearance respectful and at times was as if both women shared sorrow's affliction, one in death and one in gestation.

Each day he went out alone to the fields to work and to see what would come up the Copperhead Road. At first his mother urged the dogs on him in his daily rounds, but he wanted no warning from the dogs, either for himself or for who would come. The coming he looked for was a consequence he'd anticipated from the first time he saw the man. He carried the Springfield rifle with him and had long since determined never again would he wait to be called, to be told, to be steered in one direction or the next by any man.

On rare days he could hear rumbles coming up the mountain from across the Twelve Mile and all the way up the Copperhead Road. The sound, emanating from the dark clouds in the east, would rumble all day, and after it stopped rumbling, it would still rumble, echo over echo. At the time he did not understand the source of these detonations and explosions, but later he would learn it was the phenomenon of acoustic shadow, the traveling sound from a far distant battle skipping on air. But at the time he did not know this and thought a battle raged nearby and below and was drawn to it as if answering a call and was disquieted by these thoughts.

What he had not anticipated coming up that road was the

scavenger brother of the scavenger he'd killed behind the ear with the six-shot Remington. The morning he saw him was so quiet and still it was as if a murder had already taken place.

He was lying in the dish of an ungrained, wind-scalloped stone, high above the mountain's southern flank. He wore a blanket pulled over him and his cheek nested on the pillow of his clasped hands. Sprawls of needle-leaved juniper, knotted and stunted, scented the air. The Springfield lay beside him.

The weather was seasonal that day and it had just broke noon. He had put up dried and dented corn in the crib that morning and in the afternoon he would complete the task. He'd drunk his coffee from a jar and was eating the hard bread and pork sandwich he made for his lunch, licking the grease from his fingers. He was at his leisure, visiting with infinity, wondering what was in the rock that made it dish this way. Or was it not the rock but volition latent in the wind that slowly razored stone in so tailored and peculiar a fashion? Or was it the ancient ice his father told him about?

He was watching the mountain route that rose from the big bottom, the only way to arrive at the home place. He was nestled in a tiny high place that looked out through an ever-widening angle where it reached full degree at a hackly ridge two hundred yards very distant and then dropped off abruptly into a hollow, an inescapably tangled ravine bound with the interlocking trunks of laurel.

He had taken several deer on that ridge when they crossed and it was not so much the challenge of taking the deer but in not shooting the deer so it would carry itself over the ridge and into the jumbled back side of that ridge. His father had always warned him, You carry a deer out of there one time and you learn it's not something you ever want to do again.

And this day was different in ways other than he could describe. Rachel had not slept and he had sat up with her through the night as she seemed to hold silent conversation with what was inside her. And he felt different that morning when he loaded the Springfield and capped the revolver and filled the jar with coffee and made the meat sandwich to take with him. He did not know why, but it was in his arms and across the width of his back, his shoulder blades in particular.

He raised the brass telescope to glass again. Any other day he would have been back at work by now, but this day he lingered to watch an unfolding natural encounter on the hackly ridge.

When he had looked before, it was to see a young button-horned buck watching a red-tailed hawk perched on the open rib cage of a dead deer. The deer was old and must have broke down in the night because it'd not been there yesterday. It was different that the deer did not find a hidden place to do its dying but died there on the ridge. It is not uncommon for animals to make mistakes. Often they miscalculate in their leaps and bounds and rip their hides or break their legs. As with humans, animals are born and grow old. They are smart and some are stupid. They make mistakes. They have accidents. They live and die.

But for some reason this was different and his skin warmed with the thinking and he lingered long after it was time to return to the cornfield. He didn't know why he knew what he knew. He just knew to keep doing what he was doing.

Through the glass he watched.

The hawk was plucking shreds of intestine and gulleting them as if they were stringy worms. From the angle of his perspective the curious buck looked as if he was standing right next to the hawk rather than standing off. The bird raised its wings and flared them broad as a sail full of wind. It screamed from inside its throat. He smiled as the young buck feinted and fled.

The ridgeline was now empty except the picked carcass. It was the middle of the day and the crest of that ridge was struck with light, as if it were flint and the sunlight were steel. He had wanted to see the red-tailed hawk one more time before it flew off. He had wanted to watch it eat and take flight and pivot through the air on its powerful wings, but it'd already flown away.

Then he saw a man he recognized riding into the glass. He was riding a slowly walking horse, and though it was not the man he expected it was a man he knew, and only when he saw him did it make sense to him. The man paused within his round view to look at the carcass.

"Don't be hasty," he whispered. He spit out the gobbet of sandwich in his mouth, pressed his body to the stone, and with total certainty pulled the butt plate of the Springfield into the cradle of his shoulder. He eased the forestock onto its makeshift rest at a point behind the sling swivel and he found the blade of the front sight with the notched rear sight. He made his calculations instinctively.

When he finally left his perch he went down to find the scavenger draped on the ridgeline. He lay on his back where he'd fallen as if struck by the arm of a gigantic. His head was balding and his nose beakish. He was sunken about the eyes and his skin was pale and from where he'd fallen he was bruised yellow and purple in the face and yet even in dying he wore the hungry vulpine look.

"How's it look?" the man asked, his teeth gritted against the pain that wreaked his body.

"It ain't pretty," he said. "If that's what you are asking."

"You're a mean bastard," the scavenger muttered. "That's all you are."

"I 'magine there are some who have the exact same thing to say about you."

"I believe I asked one time your name?"

"Robey Childs," he said.

"I'll tell 'em when I get where I'm goin'."

"They'll want to know."

"Jesus, that hurts," he said. He did not motion to indicate, but clearly he spoke of the black hole in his chest.

"You ought to have been more careful," he told the man.

Blood was milking from one of the man's nostrils and in staggered moments the man did not seem to fully understand what all had happened to him. He reached his right hand in front of his face as if to clear his vision but then let it drop and his arm to dangle at his side.

"Where's my horse?" the man asked.

"He run off."

"I guess there's a lesson in this," the man said wearily, and then he said Robey's name, "Robey Childs."

"What would that lesson be?" Robey asked, but the man was now dead and thereby prevented from answering.

He made a sound with his tongue and looked to the sky. What has happened has happened, he thought, and what will happen will happen, and when that happened he'd count himself fortunate because he could get on to the next.

Overhead the thick leaves were daily turning red, orange, and yellow. The dusty water ran under black shadows and the dried corn shucks scraped and scuttled with the winglike breezes that cuffed the mountain. Those hot lovely days of July through September were now gone forever. Soon would be the driving wind, and the beating rain would become snow and the high mountains would become impassable, and in that fastness only then could he rest. He continued to stand by the scavenger's body. Why, he did not know, but felt he should do so for a while before taking his guns and whatever else of value he possessed, before toppling him over the ridge. Then he would retrieve the runaway horse and go home.

"Was it the one you'd been waiting for," his mother asked him late that night as they sat outside bundled against the chill.

"No. It weren't him."

"It was someone else," she said.

"Yes ma'am."

"How many more is there?"

"Only one," he said. "But then I thought that a'fore this one."

"I should have just had dogs," she speculated. "At least they grow up in a year."

If there was whimsy in her voice he could not detect it.

18

HEN THE END of the waiting time for the next one came it was months later and he was astride the coal black horse. They were riding the bed of the rock-bound Copperhead Road. Ice plated the slow water and eskers of snow fingered the cloud-shadowed ground.

Cold and weary, he'd come down from this day's aerie, an overlook made, he speculated, where rocks had gathered when rocks were sentient and moving, as pretime pilgrims had arrived and were exhausted from their difficult journeys and so slumped together against one another. Below this place was the concealing snow and above this place was the bottom of the wintry universe, and when he stood there he could not resist his desire to reach out with his hands in the hope he might touch them both.

The sun was lost in the sky, eclipsed by the deep cut he rode and had been so for several days, as if it was ruled by darkness this winter and so it was cold and frosted and the rock walls were blackened with frozen water. It was early evening still, and already the lights of the night had been set in motion.

The winter thus far had been the one he wished for: prolonged cold, snow and ice and a penetrating darkness that came in the late afternoon and the body never so tired as to sleep through it. There was nothing but long dark winter and the endless evergreen forest that fell from sight to the horizon miles away. There were cows to milk and feed in the wet barn and there was waiting while Rachel changed daily before his eyes as her time grew imminent.

These months spent in gestation she had remained for the most part closed to him, dark and angry and forlorn, yet she needed to be near him and always know where he was. She told him of the strange-bodied feeling of her ribs unsticking and spreading to accommodate her belly. The pains that flashed through her like wildfires. Her small bones stretching. Her faints and haunts, and sins. At times she did not seem to know where she was or how she got there or what day of the week it was and when she did know she did not care. He'd come to know fear again but not for himself. It was for how dear her life had become to him.

Last night, her voice ragged with tears, she told him she was ready to die and wanted to do so. She told him if she could not go back to the beginning she would just as soon get this life over with and be born again. He felt a shiver working into his chest bones.

The coal black horse suddenly snorted and tossed its head and scraped at the ground in stride. Robey had heard nothing odd on his own ear but retrieved the Springfield from the saddle scabbard and slipped off the road and dodged behind a dense screen of root-sprouted coppice shoots.

"This could be a bad day for someone," he said to the steady horse. Then he could hear the snow-muffled stride of a rider approaching. He did not know the outcome and that moment did not care in the least. He knew he had found what he was looking for. What would follow would be a rest of one kind or another.

He made a sound and the coal black horse rose and pitched forward into the road. The horse wheeled as he drew rein and then willfully spun in place one more rotation, jumped straight sideways, and held. He sat the horse barring the road with no perceptible movement to be seen in the hands or bit, the rifle balanced as if a scale across his lap.

The man was coming on, riding a sorrel with a white mane and four white feet. After his long search the rider was bringing conclusion as fast as he could without even knowing it. He did not stop until he brought the sorrel abreast of the crossed coal black horse.

Beyond mild surprise, the man had nothing in his eyes, but the face of him recalled the bone midden of those killing fields he'd ridden away from so many months ago, leaving his father dead and buried beneath the signifying tree. It recalled to him the night in the fire-gutted house and Rachel and the blind woman and his own head wounded by the little goose man and dressed in the torn garments of a murdered woman.

"I know you," the man said, and at first seemed pleased to have suddenly met up with him. "I been looking for you," he said.

But it went without saying. There was only one reason to be on that road and being lost wasn't likely. The man's eyes were now lively and fleeting about their sockets and it was then he determined they were not the eyes of the killer but the eyes of one fleeing sin and consequence and death.

"That's a fine horse," the man said. "Any man who'd seen that horse once would know you again."

"The hell with you," Robey told him.

"But I have caught you," the man said, setting his jaw on the words, cold and fixed. He then smiled in an attempt to take back a degree of his provocation.

"What part have I in your life?" Robey asked.

"That is what I am here to talk about."

Kill him, he thought. Put him through, he told himself, and a prefigured order of ideas deep in the map of his mind illumined as if divine. There would be no discernment, no discretion, no proportion to his justice.

"We are already dead," the man said, "you and I," and he swept a hand to indicate the high stony walls of the narrow sepulchral hollow. "Ours are the souls of the ruined," he observed with delight.

Then the shot rang out in that sunless, starless, timeless place, but by then the man was collapsed upon the neck of the sorrel horse and the unchecked horse was rising up and the man was sliding off the back of it and falling heavily to the beaten ground as if thrown down from the highest place. Midway to the snowy earth the man turned his body and folded and he landed on the point of his shoulder and with a great exhalation of pain he slumped to his back.

And it was only then the shot Robey fired across his lap was heard shattering the air.

Before dismounting he stepped the coal black horse forward and horse and rider stood over the man's fallen body. The bullet had entered his chest but had not come out. It had traveled bone and lodged in his shoulder. Eely blood trickled down his face where his skull had broke open when his head bit the stony road. An incessant groan was the best the man could do in the furor of his pain. He breathed heavily as his mind was delivered a commotion of messages that did not conflict. In his agony was the escape of his earthly and spiritual power, the tenebrous and the menace and the dark energy that ruled his life.

"I believe you hit the mark," he gasped, and tried to look down at the bubbles that pocked his chest.

"You believe that?" Robey said, dismounting and standing over him.

"Yes, I believe I do." Blood was fogging the red wheels of his glassy eyes. His colorless lips tried to shape more words, but it took several tries. "Should I not?"

"You should."

"Tell her the woman is dead. She'll want to know."

"I ain't telling her nothing," Robey said.

"My head is so heavy," the man said. "Like lead."

Nothing more was said as they waited together. He thought to feel remorse for his actions. Had he now made enough of his own needless contributions to the world's killing? No matter how just and righteous his actions? Had he not ended life the way others had ended his father's life? He thought of guilt and invited it inside himself, but it would not enter his mind or heart and it remained a cold and dormant place inside him. Did he kill himself when he first killed and so was already dead?

When his work was done he mounted the coal black horse, caught the polished reins of the sorrel, and rode toward home. As he traveled that thin stony path, he thought how a kind of

wickedness had died, but what it left behind could not be undone or unremembered. Ahead could be seen the light from
the flaring lantern shining through the windows. He thought
how the wickedness lived inside his own house but could not
be killed when it was born and must be loved without condition. He wished to shudder or tremble. He wished to regret
his actions, to lament, to cry. He wanted to long for the past
when he was a boy and lived as a boy.

But he could do none of these. His bygone days were mere
shapes and scenes played against a shadowy wall. He had no
past because he was too young. He had no past, except the
past of a child: hunger and satisfaction, heat and cold, wet and
dry, squares of yellow light on a wooden floor, companionable
animals, the love of a mother and father. There was no bite of
conscience, no thought to retrace the life and live it differently
from what was done before. He wanted nothing to do with
such wandering thoughts or feelings. He was so minded as
he rode through the evening vapors, away from the man he'd
killed beneath the moon's rising face.

That night she wandered barefoot into the room where he
sat. The only light was the nimbus of a tallow candle centered
on the table where they ate their meals.

"What is it?" she said.

"Can't sleep?" he said.

"My eyes won't close when I sleep," she said.

She stretched until her body refused to go any farther and
then she made a surprised sound and let it back. She came
close to him and tapped his knees that he should make them
a place for her to sit. She looked like a child with long tangled
lashes that wove and unwove each time her eyes closed and

opened. She scrutinized the palms of her small hands and then let them fall helplessly against the round of her belly.

"You ought to put on your stockings," he said. "The night's cold."

"It is surely cold," she said, and as if in agreement came a swoop of wind that scattered snow like buckshot against the cabin walls.

"This is the cold that brings the warm," he said, and she told him it was the same thing his mother said.

He wondered what she might be tonight. Her mind seemed improved. Would he tell her? Could he not?

"What's your idea of heaven?" she said urgently. "Do you think we are saved by hope?"

"I don't know," he said. "I don't have any answers like that tonight, nor no questions."

"Do you pray?"

"No," he said. "I don't think I do."

"Well. If you decide to start, just don't do it where I can hear it."

"I will remember that," he said.

"What is it?" she said again. "Are you going to tell me?"

"I seen him," he said, and she turned her eyes on him with all their clarity.

"You seen him?"

"He told me the woman is dead."

"Was it bad?"

"He didn't tell me and I didn't ask."

"Where'd you see him?"

"On the road. He's dead too."

She then looked off to a place that was inside her mind. He

watched her thoughts as they crossed her eyes. In her head were mysteries he could not decipher.

"Are you sure he's dead?"

"He's dead," he told her, his voice resolute, and yet he realized that even in the state of death, life-blind and quelled, the man would haunt her and he would continue his possession of her forever. He wondered if there would ever be enough peace to stop this turning for the wound that had been cut into her memory.

The room filled with a great pressure and it was as if the air was being squeezed through the cracks and jambs. The stove banged again as the fire's temperature increased and there came the visitation of memory from Gettysburg, the portal through which the past might come into the present. The stove joints ticked with expansion and a beam in the wall pealed out as it chafed on a peg. Outside the wind was running and in the morning would be white sculpted fields, the ground swept bare and strangely grassy and in other places the earth would carry hanging drifts higher than his head.

"His was the blackest soul," she said as if the news of his death was all so long ago.

She held out her hand, a fist unfolded, her mouth open and wordless. For days she'd struggled to find the strength to bear down on the pain. She thought she must get it stopped before it continued. For days she'd felt her tiny bones shifting and moving, finding positions of accommodation. She prayed for the strength, but it just hadn't come. She suddenly groaned and cried out as her leg was seized by a cramp. She stretched the curled leg and held it in the air above the floor where its muscle quivered beneath her skin and finally loosened. The infant was ready to be born, and known only to her it was rushing its birth.

"The pain when it comes is worse than knives," she said. "I want to die." Then she said, "Lift me up," and when he did she said, "Come to bed," and he followed her to bed where she asked he lay down behind her and press his knuckled hand against her back.

"Don't rub," she said, her voice reed thin. "Just push hard. Push as hard as you can with your fist."

When the pain subsided she wanted him to hold her in his arms and rock her gently. He found the back of her neck with his face and breathed deeply her sleepy smell. She moved her back into his chest and pulled his arm to her chest, his hand to her breast. There was about nothing left of her, not back or shoulders or chest, her belly so huge. She moved his hand to her belly and there her skin was stretched and taut and it was holding her this way they slipped into the lull of exhausted sleep.

He did not remember when he fell asleep but his gesture upon waking was to resume the pushing with his fist. Yet when he lifted his hand he found nothing to touch and when he crawled up through sleep, he could not find her and the bed was cold and soaking wet. He stood from the wet bed and with his first drink of water rinsed the taste of sleep from his mouth and with the second slaked the thirst brought on by the dry heat of the wood fire. He thought to have found her in the darkness by now, but he didn't.

Then he called out to her and tore the quilt from the bed and barefoot he was running for the door.

Outside the night was blue and vivid and continuous with

its blanket of scraping winter light. He could hear his mother come from sleep and calling out his name at his back. In the forest the pines wore their mantles of snow and from the barns and stables was drafted a strange and serene silence. He called out her name in the stillness and the sound of his voice ran out to distance across the brow of the snow-covered summit.

"Rachel," he cried. "Rachel."

He felt the sting of cold in his lungs. His heart was pounding in his chest, but there was no answer returned. In the sky Pegasus was due west and the Big Dipper stood upright on its handle. The flight silhouette of an owl, its shallow wing beats passed over his head and he looked off in its telling direction.

Then he could see her in faint illumination lighted by the moon. She lay at the misted and unfrozen stream bank, where she'd carried herself to the place where the hot waters bubbled up from the earth. She was trembling and moaning and he began to run to her, but when she saw him coming she stood. She held up a hand and yelled at him, "Let me die," but she did not speak whole words before they were torn with her cries of pain. He kept on, dragging the blanket he'd pulled from the bed. She waved her hands, no, telling him to stay away, and when he did not stop she turned and threw herself full body into the warm water.

He saw the flash of her white legs as she fell down into the pool. He was running across the frozen ground, so near the clouded and steamy shoals of the spring. She then stood upright, her wet shift a sheen in the moonlight and stepped into the eddy where the current circled a boulder before taking a sharp cooling swing, before quickening and roping with heavy turbulence and troughy rapids, before falling off the mountain.

Here she let go from her grasp and there was a white bobbing that floated from the shallows and made for the current's catch. There was first one and then there was another one and both of them dunking and rising like tiny pumpkins, the second one floating after the first one.

He splashed into the shallows of the birth-stained water as the current carried them toward the falls. He threw himself forward, rasing a great flounce of water that swiftly closed to submerge him. He stood and ran and dove again, his thighs breaking the surface, and he was catching them in his hands, first one and then the other, their tiny faces red and soundless and contorted with the unimaginable terror of being born.

Afterward, he wished to console her, but she seemed to want nothing from him. She turned her back on him and in her stance was written the question why: Why did you do that? Why did you save them? Who gave you the right to do that?

She told him, "I want to hate you for what you have done, hate you as much as I hate him who did this to me," but he made no reply.

For several days there was nothing of motherhood that kindled inside her, but Hettie would not relent and finally she gave in and let them nurse at her breasts. They were two little boys with fine downy birth-hair on their shoulders, backs, and their odd-shaped heads. Their faces were like those of tiny old men and they beat the air with their fists and their cries were hearty and healthy exercises. She refused to name them and they were not concerned because for this there would be time.

Then there was more cold and a chilling rain that turned to snow and lasted for days, and winter on the mountain that year seemed longer and colder than any winter before. The snow and cold, as if an edgeless sea, enveloped the dormant earth, the arrowed pines shrugged to the skirling wind. Hung in the sky was the white sun, the desolate glistering of far bright stars, the cooling remnants of old stars. Outside the candle-bright cabin was a tide of white-locked fields in deep suspended silence.

During these days of snow-pent darkness he was seized by a sleep with an iron grip, senseless, nameless, and peaceful sleep, and only afterward did he sense the flow of time gone by and feel what was inside him begin to ease. He had died a first death and a second and a third. He knew in this life he was not done with death and killing.

It was a sleeper's world frosted, silent, dark and starkly beautiful, and he remembered tranquillity. He remembered the days in the valley riding the coal black horse. The horse rising to the bit, its hot breath blowing back at him, the shedding sweat from its sleek black neck, flecks of foam from its quivering nostrils. He remembered his father. He remembered the dead. He remembered nothing moving in the darkness of those nights, but one night he awoke to a chorus of baby cries and Rachel cradling a baby in her arms and feeding the baby and then feeding the other baby, and when she lay down she lay down beside him, her belly tucked against his back and her face at his neck. He remembered her arm reaching across his chest and gently taking her wrist in his hand. Sleep, he remembered thinking, sleep a little while longer.

COAL

BLACK

HORSE

A Conversation with the Author

A Reading and Discussion Guide

Although the novel is largely about a boy's journey, it is also about a very particular moment in history. Much of its power comes from the Civil War battle scenes, which feel so real and visceral. What kind of research did you do to re-create those scenes?

It began with a visit to Gettysburg. As a boy growing up in New Hampshire, my war of fascination was the American Revolution, but when living in southern Pennsylvania I began to wonder about the Civil War. So I went to Gettysburg to see the battlefield and slowly but surely began to feel myself drawn into that experience. I was trying, as a curious person, to learn about it and understand it. I began to read and one thing led to another. I visited other battlefields and somewhere along the way I decided I wanted to try to write this novel. Again, as a way to experience it. I was as ignorant of this world as Robey Childs and in a sense I invented him so that we could discover it together. I remember I was at Shiloh for a major reenactment and was standing inside a battery of cannons. I could feel the concussive force of the explosions against my body and coming up through the earth. My face felt wet and when I wiped at my nose it was bleeding. I thought how that must have happened to the artillerists and for a moment I had the tiniest glimpse of their experience.

You're not from the South, yet you capture your characters' voices and diction so well. Did you read Civil War accounts or did it come by way of instinct?

It's true, I'm not Southern born but was raised in the country in the northern reach of the Appalachian chain. A lot of similarities up north and down south along that spine of those mountains. And the mountains of West Virginia, the fictional setting of Robey's home, exists in a kind of not-south not-north ether. Even in ancient times it was a place where the northern tribes and southern tribes brushed up against each other and was a kind of no-man's-land, contested territory and a place where you could get killed. As to the voices, I think of them as rural and arcadian, naturally sardonic, and trenchant. My family had an amazing talent for the aphoristic and the epigrammatic. This went a long way in establishing authority in a character. When Hettie Childs first spoke she came onto the page as if she'd been waiting 150 years and finally this was her moment. She is real to me in every way.

It seems as though the coal black horse is equally real to you. Did you grow up with horses?

Horses, cows, pigs, sheep. Yes. The farm is still there and I get home every chance I can. The coal black horse began as a simple means of conveyance. The boy needed a good horse if he was to carry out his mother's imperative. He needed a horse with experience he lacked. So I came up with the coal black horse and then the strangest thing happened. With each draft the horse became more and more prominent. The horse grew in my mind and grew on the page and in time the horse was the same to me as it was to Robey Childs. I mean that literally. Such a horse as I imagined was lustrously iridescent. Like coal when turned to the light. I was amazed when I first saw the hardcover jacket my publisher did for the hardcover. It is so arresting. It really took my breath away. And of course there is something ancient and timeless about the horse and the rider. The horse is consort and for thousands of years we have lived together by agreement. I think they are very beautiful. Sometimes I think, like Hettie, the coal black horse was out there the whole time and just waiting for Robey and me to come along.

In the process of writing the book, did you think about how warfare has changed since the Civil War?

Combat actually changed during that war. Take for instance the minie ball, invented by Captain Claude-Étienne Minié of France. This was a high-caliber grooved conical lead bullet. It could be loaded quickly, and because it was grooved, when fired from a rifle it was very accurate over a long distance, and yet the generals still believed in massed lines of men in close formation charging over open ground. New weapons, old tactics. Wounds were especially horrible and so many wounded required amputation because the minie ball did not just break bone but actually shattered whole sections of bone, and the bone could not be mended.

But however terrible and chaotic war is, I think instances of courage and dignity and sacrifice in warfare are timeless and universal. I am not sure if it's true, but I read that the men who retreated after Pickett's famous charge walked backwards because it would have been ignoble to have been shot in the back.

Even now I think the reasons why boys and men go to war haven't changed. We must recognize what a great adventure war is. If not for the Civil War thousands and thousands of young men were destined to live their entire lives in the same place, the same town. They saw the war as an escape from daily lives that were relentlessly boring and tedious. War is extremely liberating and purifying and for so many men, they were never so alive as when they were at war. It is not acceptable to talk about this love of war, but I think it's real. I do not think this has changed. William Faulkner wrote, "The past is never dead. It's not even past."

What was the biggest challenge for you in writing the novel?

I think all writers are more interested in what they don't know than what they do know. Naturally, helplessly, hopelessly curious about everything. Research is so fascinating. I just loved all that reading and those experiences, but ultimately I am a dramatist, not a historian. So, two things: First I had to acknowledge how inexhaustible the information is and literally begin to turn away from it. Second, I had to find a way to animate the story I wanted to tell. But, where to start? And how to start? And where to go from there? In a sense, all stories are about what we mean to ourselves and what we mean to each other. It's really that simple, but every one of them has to be different. I thought about the boy leaving home and entering that landscape. He was really quite the innocent. He was born in remoteness. It was his story I wanted to tell—a boy sent out to bring his father home, a boy looking for his father. I think for all time mothers have been sending their sons to bring home their fathers. I think about how hard it was for her to send him. I assumed a vein of iron in these people. I think there are people who have such faith in each other.

Your characters do seem to retain faith under very difficult circumstances. Did any of them surprise you?

Yes, late in the novel, at Gettysburg when Robey takes justice into his own hands. I remember the days when writing that scene. I do not approve of what he did, but I could not stop him. It was as if his will was discovered and he became a powerful influence in every rewrite thereafter, and there were quite a few. Hettie seemed to come onto the page all at once and it was only afterward that I realized how powerful her presence is throughout the book. She is present in the opening and the ending, but for me she was never very far away. She possessed a kind of strength and wisdom and equanimity that the world so lacked. And of course the coal black horse becoming more prominent by increments until finally it became the title. I still have dreams about them.

Are there any other characters who are entering your dreams? Is there another novel unfolding in your mind?

I have never thought of writing as something I do but as a place where I go. There I find a community and a language and an experience of totality. So, yes. The event at the end of

Coal Black Horse, the birth. When I first realized that Rachel was pregnant, I felt an overwhelming responsibility and only later, when she eventually gives birth, did I know she was having twins. As I have mentioned, there are days you remember when you are working and these were two of them: her being pregnant and then having twins. I just couldn't let that go, so in the book I'm working on now, I am telling their story, only it is years and years later and they are grown men.

1. Why do you think Robey's mother sends him on a dangerous journey to find his father? How do you feel about her
   decision?

2. Robey is reminded of his mother as he travels. For example, when he is shot: "He was in pain and his mother always said that pain was weakness leaving the body" (page
   53). Where else in the story do you find her presence? How
   would you characterize their relationship?

3. In what ways does the landscape at the farm, on the road,
   on the battlefield, and in Gettysburg inform the story and
   affect Robey and the people around him?

4. In his travels Robey sees a lot of strange, beautiful, and
   gruesome things. For example, the horse skeleton covered
   with vines and flowers (page 26) and then the description
   of the man's skeleton a few pages later (page 29). What
   other examples of this juxtaposition can you find? How do
   they affect how you understand Robey's journey?

5. Robey meets so many characters on the road—Morphew,
   the German, the upside-down boy, the goose man, the major, the pregnant woman in the graveyard, the scavenger

brothers. How do these secondary characters help (or impair) Robey's quest to find his father?

6. What role do fate and second sight play in the novel? For example, Robey's mother knows that Thomas Jackson has died without being told and that Robey must find his father before July. What other examples can you find, and how do fate and premonition guide your own life?

7. Morphew tells Robey that he is "in for an education" (page 21). After a battle later in the story, Robey has this encounter with the coal black horse (page 112): "Then he urged the horse on and it hesitated before responding as if to acknowledge that its rider had learned some valuable lesson and should be rewarded for such." What is Robey learning? How does he acknowledge his education?

8. Throughout the course of the novel Robey has to make hard decisions such as stealing food and horses. How does he feel about these decisions? In what ways do they seem to change him?

9. Robey doesn't kill the man who rapes Rachel even though he has the opportunity and cause to do so. Why doesn't he?

10. Religion plays a significant role over the course of the story, perhaps most dramatically in this revelation on page 116: "He decided from that day forever after that there must live a heartless God to let such despair be visited on the earth, or as his father said, a God too tired and no longer capable of doing the work required of him." How do religion and spirituality shape the novel?

11. Pages 124–26 describe the scavengers and minor businesses that spring up in the wake of battle. How does Robey seem to feel about this? How does this affect your perception of the Civil War?

12. The pregnant woman in the graveyard tells Robey that "people should be born twice: once as they are and once as they are not" (page 130). What does she mean by this? How does this tie into the themes of the novel?

13. How would you describe Robey's relationship with his mother, the coal black horse, his father, and Rachel? How is each relationship different and alike? And how do these relationships define Robey as a boy and Robey as a man?

14. War has affected the land and the people—for example, the "raggedy old woman with a sun-stained and stroke-twisted face" (page 178). To what extent have the characters, the land, and even the animals been affected by the ravages of of war?

15. How does the birth of the twins change Robey? How does it change Rachel? Do you have the sense that things will be better or worse for the family? Why?

16. How has Robey's story altered the way you think about war and violence? Has it made you think about love and faith differently? Are there particular passages that reflect your opinions and feelings?

MOLLY ULINE-OLMSTEAD

ROBERT OLMSTEAD is the author of five previous books (*River Dogs, Soft Water, A Trail of Heart's Blood Wherever We Go, America by Land,* and *Stay Here with Me*). The recipient of a Guggenheim fellowship, an NEA grant, and the 2007 Heartland Award for Fiction, he is a professor at Ohio Wesleyan University.